MY ONE AND ONLY
Copyright © 2019 Alanea Alder

PUBLISHER'S NOTE
This is a work of fiction. Any names, characters, places and incidents are the product of the author's imagination or are used fictiously, and any resemblance to actual persons, living or dead, business establishments, events or locales is entirely coincidental.

www.sacredforestpublishing.com
P.O.Box 280
Moyock, NC, 27958
Digital ISBN- 978-1-941315-22-4
Print ISBN- 978-1-941315-23-1
Sacred Forest Publishing
Cover Design and Interior Format

MY
ONE AND ONLY

BEWITCHED AND BEWILDERED

ALANEA ALDER

DEDICATION

~Omnia Vincit Amor-Love Conquers All~

"Because tomorrow isn't promised."
~Serenity Meadowsweet~

PROLOGUE

MICAH'S EYES BLURRED FROM LACK of sleep. His patrols were on Level Five today with Warrick. He fully planned on hitting every vendor dealing in caffeine on Level Six before reporting in.

He stared up at the false night sky in his garden. What he wouldn't give for just one single moment with his mate. If Fate kept her away and kept her safe, he knew that if he were given just one moment he could face a life without her.

Please, he begged. *One moment to last a lifetime.*

CHAPTER ONE

MICAH WALKED BETWEEN MERYN AND Warrick as they waved to the skittish people on Level Five. Ryuu followed behind them, an ever-present shadow to his charge.

"They look like they're about to piss themselves," Meryn observed when level residents hurried into their homes, slamming their doors, when the trio walked past them down the long corridor back toward the transport tunnel.

Warrick sighed. "I knew it had gotten bad, but not this bad."

Micah nodded. "I've patrolled Level Five before, but you know we stay pretty close to the tunnel. It's been a long-standing custom for any citizen with a problem to meet with us there, I never really second-guessed it." He looked around. "I'm wondering how many of these people were allowed anywhere near the tunnel."

Meryn turned her face up at him. "Why not patrol the whole level?"

Micah's eyes widened. "Meryn, that would be like walking an entire city. I mean we're good, but we're not that good."

Meryn blinked. "Oh yeah, the beehive thing."

Micah chuckled. "The city isn't structured like a beehive."

"Whatever."

Micah was about to tease her some more when a small figure stepped out in front of them. He and Warrick exchanged pained expressions. They were familiar with this particular resident. He was an adorable menace, molded by his father to be a thorn in their sides. None of the warriors would ever hurt the little guy, but that didn't mean he wasn't a nuisance. When you're trained to take down ferals, a young vampire half your size wasn't much of a threat.

Micah looked between the young man and Warrick, he doubted that even standing on tiptoe he reached Warrick's sternum.

"You were banned from here. Go away. Shoo." The elf-like young man said making a 'shooing' motion with his hands.

Meryn tilted her head. "Huh? Warrick is the Founding Family head here now. So like the ban is totally a moot point."

"It is not muted or quiet," the dark-haired youngster countered.

"No. Moot, not mute. It means not valid any-more, not that the sound was cut," she explained.

The young man's eyes filled with confusion. "He did not tell me that."

"Who?" Meryn asked.

"My father."

Meryn looked up at him. "His father?"

Micah pointed to the man in front of them.

"Meryn McKenzie, this is Pip Maverick. DeLa-Fontaine's biological son."

Meryn's eyes widened. "Gavriel said that DeLaFontaine didn't have any heirs or anyone to succeed him."

Warrick winced. "Technically he does not. Pip was never listed in the DeLaFontaine Book of Life."

Meryn frowned. "Why not?"

Pip blushed fiercely. "Because I was born damaged," he whispered.

"Well that's bullshit. I mean you don't look damaged." Meryn eyed him closely.

Pip looked at her surprised. "I do not?"

She shook her head. "Nope, you look normal to me."

"Father says I am slow. That he should have drowned me at birth," Pip admitted shamefully.

"Not to sound mean or anything but your dad is a huge asshole," Meryn said.

Pip's eyes widened and he looked around frantically. "You should not say such things. They will take you away to face my father."

Meryn snorted. "I'd like to see them try." She pointed to Warrick then behind her to Ryuu. "Warrick is in charge of this level, everyone answers to him now. And if anyone tried to take me away my squire would gut them."

"Most certainly *denka*," Ryuu confirmed behind them.

"I do not want you to get hurt. You are nice and explained things to me." Pip started to rock back and forth while his two small fists pounded his temples. "But Father told me I had to chase you away no matter what, even if I had to do bad things."

Meryn looked at them panicked. "Help him," she commanded.

Warrick quickly got down on one knee and gently took Pip's fists into his own large hands. "Pip, how do you know that your father wants you to be mean?"

Pip sniffed. "He told me during my last visit."

Warrick looked at Micah then back to Pip. "You visit your father?"

Pip nodded. "I am the only one who gets to see him since we are blood related."

"That may explain how the tunnel escort got instructions," Micah murmured.

Warrick nodded his head slightly to acknowledge that he heard him. "Pip, did you give anyone instructions on behalf of your father?"

Pip nodded slowly, fear in his eyes. "Was I bad? Am I in trouble?"

Micah was seeing a new side of Pip. Normally the tiny vampire would just throw things at them or yell things from the side streets. Maybe his previous behavior hadn't been his own doing after all.

Warrick shook his head. "No, you are not bad, nor are you in trouble." Warrick turned back to look at Micah and Meryn. "What do we do?"

Micah knew what Warrick meant. With DeLaFontaine in the detention cells he wasn't sure anyone was looking out for the young vampire. He wasn't even sure that Pip knew how to fly he appeared to be too young.

Meryn stepped forward. "Pip, if you could do anything, what would make you happy?"

Pip's blue eyes grew wide. "Anything?"

Warrick smiled. "Yes, anything."

Pip smiled brightly transforming his entire face into something close to angelic. "I do not want to be mean anymore or do bad things. I want someplace safe to sleep and..." he hesitated.

"And," Warrick prodded gently.

"Food. Food whenever I am hungry," Pip admitted softly.

Meryn pushed Warrick's hands out of the way and wrapped an arm around Pip. "He's mine for as long as he wants me."

Warrick stood. "Now, Meryn."

She turned to face them eyes flashing. "No. I'm not saying it's y'all's fault, but this must have been going on for years." She pinned them both with an angry glare. "You want to help?" She waved around her. "Fix this shit. You're unit warriors designated to protect people, start protecting." She turned to Pip. "Come on little buddy. You're staying with me for a while."

"I am?" Pip asked. "What do I have to do?"

Meryn shrugged. "Keep me company and help me eat Sebastian's food."

Pip subconsciously licked his lips. "Eat?"

Meryn's eyes had a sheen to them. She swallowed hard before smiling at him. "Yup. He's going to love you. He lives to feed people." She tugged on his hand. "Come on."

Pip hesitated turning back to Warrick. "You are really the Founding Family head now?" Meryn waited as Pip asked for clarification.

Warrick nodded. "I am."

"Do I have to see my father anymore?"

"No. Not if you do not want to."

"Do I have to be bad anymore?"

"No."

"Am I allowed to use the transport tunnel and go with Meryn?"

"Any citizen in this city is allowed to use the transport tunnel," Warrick answered looking confused.

"Do I have to come back?" Pip asked quietly.

"Nope," Meryn answered. "In fact if you want to swing by your place and pick up your things you won't have to come back ever."

Pip shook his head back and forth. "I am not allowed to own things."

Meryn grinned. "You can now."

Pip straightened. "I want to go with Meryn and eat Sebastian food."

Warrick nodded and smiled. "Have fun."

As they walked away Micah could see that Meryn had a death grip on Pip's hand. Ryuu stepped between him and Warrick. "I am assuming you will do everything in your power to help Pip's situation?"

Warrick sighed. "Of course. Him and everyone else on Level Five."

Ryuu nodded tersely. "You have no idea how much his plight aligns with Meryn's childhood. In her heart she already considers him family and thus I consider him one of my charges." He met their eyes and smiled frostily. "I really do not wish to kill anyone while I am here... but I will if I have to." He bowed to them and quickly caught up to Meryn who was explaining Magic Pudding to a mesmerized Pip.

When they cleared the tunnel Warrick let out an explosive breath. "Gods! If I did not think that taking the Founding Family head position would keep Avery safer, I would happily tell Gavriel I decline the prestigious promotion."

"Better you than me," Micah teased.

Warrick gave him a sour look. "Where do I even begin to sort out this clusterfuck of a level?"

Micah thought about it for a moment. "Why don't you do what Kari did? Meet with the Noble Family heads and have them help trickle down information and policy change."

"Have you forgotten that the uncle who disowned me, is one of the Noble Family heads who now report to me?" he asked.

Micah blinked then laughed. "I had forgotten that."

Warrick rubbed his chin. "LeBeau is not that bad. But I have a feeling that my uncle will try to sabotage me at every turn."

Micah shrugged. "So replace him."

Warrick stared at him in shock. "We cannot do that!"

"Why not? It's how you got promoted."

"The circumstances surrounding my promotion were unique, impossible and extreme."

Micah stepped closer and cast a soundproof bubble. "Look. Meryn is right. There's a ton of shady shit going on around here that's been happening right under our noses and we missed it because we had to kowtow to tradition. Well you know what? Fuck that. We finally have a free pass and his name is freaking Dark Prince Gavriel Ambrosios. The entire city of Noctem Falls genuflects when someone mentions his name and for good reason. If your uncle gives you shit, tell Gavriel and get permission to have him replaced. Gavriel can do no wrong. We have a very small window of opportunity to finally help people. Take it." Micah exhaled.

Warrick simply stared at him. "You are right." He straightened then gave him a wolfish grin. "Let us head to Level One, check on Pip, then possibly meet with Gavriel about reorganizing some of the Noble Families."

Micah took down the soundproofing spell. "After you," Micah swept his arm down as he bowed.

"You know if I get to do what I want, I will need back up," Warrick murmured.

"It would be a profound honor and pleasure to assist you in that endeavor. In fact, I bet Declan and his brother Rex would also love to help, considering recent events."

Warrick laughed loudly. "And Declan says we never do anything nice for him."

Micah grinned. "Ungrateful bastard."

Laughing Warrick slung an arm around his shoulder as they walked toward the transport tunnel.

As far as patrols went, today was shaping up to be a great day.

"Are you sure about this?" Radclyffe asked for the tenth time that hour.

Serenity Meadowsweet blew out an exasperated breath. "For the umpteenth time, no, I am not sure, but I'm going anyway."

"You mean we're all going." Radclyffe Juniper pointed his finger back and forth between himself and his mate Laelia.

"You don't have to come, in fact, it might be a better idea for the two of you to stay behind and manage the temple," Serenity suggested, pausing in her packing efforts.

"Don't be silly. You need us," her closest friend rebutted. Laelia Juniper was one of the sweetest women she had ever met. She wanted her friend's support desperately but knew that if they followed her to Noctem Falls, they could all get in serious trouble.

Serenity zipped her bag closed. She hadn't packed much, just a few changes of clothes. They would be providing magical support so there wasn't much to pack as far as supplies went. She turned to face her two best friends. "You realize that by coming with me to Noctem Falls we are going against the Witch Elders' dictate concerning Storm Keep's participation in this crisis?" They both nodded. "And by coming with me all three of us could be prosecuted when we return?" Again, they nodded.

Laelia swung her bag onto her shoulder and her mate did the same. "Not only are we not letting you do this alone, but we also happen to agree with you that it is our duty to provide help." She waved her hand around indicating to the room. "You're the Head of the Water Temple in Storm Keep. We're the hub for healing magic in the paranormal world. If we don't go, then who will?"

Radclyffe adjusted his bag. "Besides, if we weren't meant to help then there wouldn't be a Healer's

Clause built into the quarantine protocols for the fae portals."

Serenity was shocked when the queen of the fae reached out to her directly to ask if she was willing to enact the clause and go to Noctem Falls to assist in fighting the unknown sickness. The fae were unable to pass through to the vampire city, but the queen explained that if a portal was opened from within the Water Temple, healers could pass through to provide assistance.

Serenity had been honest with the queen when she said she wasn't sure what she should do, wanting to get her Elders' permission first. As a temple head she reported directly to the Witch Elder Council that ran the city. She had a feeling that if the city's council, consisting of the four major races, had been included in the decision making, she would have been allowed to go.

Queen Aleksandra said the decision was up to her and that she wouldn't advise anyone in Noctem Falls about the possibility of her coming until she made up her mind.

Serenity knew she wanted to help and thought that going before the council would be a formality. She had been shocked by their unanimous decision to let the vampires of Noctem Falls fend for themselves.

When she returned to the temple she knew she had to act quickly. She immediately called her brother and had him leave Eiré Danu through a portal to come to Storm Keep. He would be the one to open the portal to Noctem Falls for them. She wanted to keep the queen out of this traitorous venture as much as possible. No one would second guess her older brother Zachari coming to visit her, they were twins after all and visited each other often.

Serenity picked up her bag. "I'm leaving Troy in charge while we're gone."

Radclyffe nodded. "Great choice. He is as devoted to you as temple head as he is to rules and regulations. He can easily handle the council."

"Knock, knock. Seri, where are you?" a deep male voice asked. Moments later her brother was ducking his head to walk into her chambers. When he saw her, his smile widened. "There's my favorite baby sister!" He crossed the room and pulled her into a bear hug that had her spine cracking.

Despite being twins they looked nothing alike. He took after their fae father. Tall, golden and stunning. The two differences between him and full blooded fae males were the streaks of dark brown hair, visible even when pulled back in a ponytail as he usually wore it, and the dark brown eyes he inherited from their mother. Dark eyes amongst the fae were highly unusual.

She took after their witch mother with dark hair and magical gifts. However, unlike her brother she had their father's lavender eyes. Her mother always said that the two of them were the perfect blend of witch and fae.

Zach had some powers but not enough to warrant being tested by the Magical Academy. He cheekily told her that he could do just enough magic to keep his lady friends happy. She told him that she didn't need to know any more.

To make living in Storm Keep easier she took her mother's maiden name of Meadowsweet forgoing fae tradition. No matter what rules she bent or broke growing up she always had her parents full support. She could only hope they wouldn't be too upset at her for going against council dictates.

"Zach! Put me down," she laughed. No matter how long they were ever apart he always greeted her this way. He set her down on her feet, his face turning serious.

"Are you sure about going? I don't want to you falling ill."

"From what the queen told me so far it's only affecting shifters and vampires. Many witch unit warriors have been helping the sick and none of them have been infected. They need our help. It's what we've studied for," she answered.

He rubbed his chin. "I don't like it."

"You don't have to, you just have to open the portal."

"Even though we're twins you can't open a portal and I can," he shook his head. "Genetics are weird."

"I can split a river and you can't," she countered.

He grinned. "You've improved. When we were kids you had problems with mud puddles," he teased.

She gave him a flat look. "I *am* a temple head now."

"Yes mistress temple head, anything you say mistress temple head," Zach bowed low, his fingertips brushing the floor.

Serenity rolled her eyes. "You're impossible!"

Zach looked up and winked. "But you love me anyway." He straightened then turned to Laelia. "And how is my second favorite lady?"

Laelia blushed. "I am well."

Radclyffe shook his head. He was used to Zach's teasing. "You never greet me like that."

Zach looked surprised for a moment then leered at both of them. "If I didn't know how in love the two of you were I'd seduce you both."

"Zach!" Serenity screeched.

He turned to her frowning. "Have you been studying with a banshee?"

"Open the damn portal then go home!" she pointed to the blank wall of her chambers.

"I am never appreciated," he sighed. "I may hide out in Storm Keep for a bit. Allia Li'Aerlin wants to 'train'. She's been a bear to work with since she wasn't able to send her brother any troops, if she finds out I opened a portal to Noctem Falls she'll attack me in my sleep," he groused.

Laelia and Radclyffe were fighting back laughter as they walked over to stand next to Serenity.

"Allia and Ailain both spoil you since we're the next set of twins born after them in Eiré Danu," Serenity pointed out.

He rolled his eyes. "Being nearly three hundred isn't very old in the paranormal world, but in Eiré Danu it's a thousand times worse. I feel like a damn toddler."

"You are one of the youngest in a city of immortals," Serenity teased.

Zach gave her a flat look before opening the pouch at his waist to pull out a silver ring. "Her Majesty appreciates your attempts to protect her by keeping her out of this venture. That being said, she lent me this ring. It should open a portal directly to the Ledge of Noctem Falls. When the portal opens it will also bypass the spell that hides the door and open it for you. To pass through the portal you have to be a witch. I think it scans for magic to prove you're a healer." His handsome face sobered. "Be careful Seri. Don't hesitate to call if you need help. I'll chance going through the portal with my meager magical abilities to get to you."

Serenity hugged her brother tightly. "Love you."

He gave her one last squeeze and stepped back. "Love you too. Have fun breaking the law."

She gave him a salute then turned to face the wall. Zach slipped on the ring and opened the portal. "Gods' blessings be on you all," he whispered as they walked through.

Micah thought that if Pip's eyes widened any-more they would simply fall out of his head. The poor boy had no idea how to take Meryn. Currently she was trying to get him to sit next to her in a chair. Micah looked around the dining room. "Where's Sebastian?"

Ryuu lifted Pip from where he was kneeling on the floor and sat him next to Meryn. "He is check-ing on Magnus." He looked down at the young vampire. "Sit next to Meryn if you would please. It would hurt her back to keep leaning down to look at you," he explained gently.

Pip's eyes filled with understanding. "I would not want to hurt Meryn." Of course he would sit next to Meryn for her own sake, not because he wanted to sit on the furniture. "The servants in my father's home usually put my bowl on the floor," he explained.

"They what?" a terribly cold voice asked. Micah was shocked to see that the question came from the normally pleasant Sebastian.

The Rioux squire walked into the room to stand behind Meryn and Pip. "Who is this?" he asked.

Meryn pointed to her new friend. "This is Pip, DeLaFontaine was his sperm donor. As you heard, he's done a bang up job of taking care of him." She looked up at the squire her eyes pleading. "He's hungry Sebastian."

Sebastian inhaled and looked down at the innocent face staring up at him. "Well, we cannot have that can we? Give me a few minutes to throw something together."

Meryn gave him a thumbs up. Pip held up his hand and curled his fingers down to give the squire a thumbs up sign as well. Sebastian patted them both on the head and quickly headed to the kitchen.

Meryn sighed. "Being hungry sucks."

Micah had a feeling she wasn't just referring to the annoying rumbling you get between breakfast and lunch. The look in her eyes told a darker story.

Pip nodded. "It makes it hard to sleep."

"Even though you're tired and want to sleep your body keeps telling you to eat," Nigel said quietly.

Meryn looked at the twins that sat on her other side. "You too?"

Neil smiled weakly. "Sometimes there wasn't a lot of food at the orphanage, so we gave ours to the little kids."

Micah could only stare. His childhood hadn't been all roses and puppies but his grandmother made sure he had never gone without.

Meryn shook her head as if to chase away her thoughts. "Yup. But we don't have to worry about that now. We have Ryuu and Sebastian to feed us."

The twins smiled. "They rock!"

Pip turned to the witches. "Do you belong to Meryn too?"

Nigel laughed. "She adopted us as her brothers."

"Brothers? Not servants?" Pip tilted his head.

"What?" Meryn asked frowning.

"Did you not bring me here for me to serve you?" Pip asked.

"No! I wasn't kidding when I said I just wanted you to keep me company. If that's not what you want, you can do whatever. I don't see you as a servant." She jerked her thumb toward Ryuu. "I can barely handle having one."

Pip twisted his hands nervously. "I do not understand. What am I supposed to do to earn my food?"

Meryn's mouth opened and closed. "Ryuu? I need some help here."

Ryuu stepped closer to stand behind Meryn and Pip. "Master Pip, my charge views you as someone to be protected. She does not require payment for things such as clothes and food. You bring her happiness by simply accepting her kindness. If you feel you must do something in return, help me watch over her and keep her safe."

Pip nodded quickly. "I can do that. Meryn is nice. Bad things should not happen to her."

"You will do very well here," Ryuu said smiling.

"Are we keeping him?" Nigel asked his eyes

filled with tears.

Meryn nodded. "He's one of us now."

"This is awesome! We now have another brother!"

"What?" a deep voice asked.

Aiden strode into the room scowling. Immediately Pip popped out of his chair to stand in front of Meryn. He stretched out his arms. "You will not hurt her."

Aiden stopped dead in his tracks and stared down at the young man who was about the size of one of his legs. "Huh?"

Meryn giggled. "Pip that's my mate Aiden McKenzie. He would never hurt me, I have access to his unconscious body."

Aiden rolled his eyes. "And you love me."

"And I love you," she added.

Behind Aiden everyone else began to file in for lunch.

Pip eyed Aiden suspiciously. He made a 'V' with his fingers and pointed to his eyes. "I will keep an eye on you." He sat back down in his chair and scooted closer to Meryn.

Aiden's mouth dropped as Colton burst into laughter. "Better sleep with one eye open tonight."

Aiden snarled at his best friend then realized that Pip was in his chair. Grumbling he sat down next to the odd vampire and one seat down from his mate.

"Who's the cutie?" Anne asked.

"Anne, everyone, this is Pip Maverick, my newest brother. DeLaFontaine is his sperm donor," Meryn announced.

Aiden inhaled and began to choke on his breadstick. "What? Again?"

"Yup." Meryn gave a single decisive nod.

"But you already have Jaxon, Noah, Nigel and Neil," Aiden stuttered.

"And? I can't have another brother?" Meryn asked.

"I think he is absolutely adorable," Bethy added.

Meryn turned to Pip. "Beth adopted me as her sister, so technically y'all are related too."

Pip turned his large liquid-like blue eyes to Bethy. "She's so pretty."

"Oh!" Bethy blushed then blinked. "DeLaFontaine?"

"Caught that did you?" Micah asked raising an eyebrow.

Bethy turned to Gavriel. "I thought you said he didn't have any heirs."

Gavriel stared at Pip frowning. "He does not. Pip's name is not in the DeLaFontaine Book of Life."

"Because I am broken," Pip whispered.

"You are not!" Bethy said indignantly.

Pip raised his head and looked around. "Really? Everyone in my father's home said I was good for nothing."

"That's why you don't live there anymore remember?" Meryn pointed out.

Pip's face contorted in confusion. "Then why did they say such things? Why did they do bad things?"

"Because they are assholes. Trust me, the world is full of them," Meryn said sagely.

Pip looked around nervously. "If you say bad things the men will take you away."

Meryn shook her head. "Not down here."

"I would like to see them try to take you or Miss

Meryn away," Sebastian said darkly as he wheeled in a huge cart piled high with food. He steered it over to Pip first. "I did not know what you liked so I made bit of everything. Sandwiches, soup, finger foods, and even a pizza." He leaned down. "Save room for dessert," he said winking.

Pip's eyes locked on the cart. "I do not get served first," he said in a panicked voice. "I get the left-overs in my bowl on the floor." Pip looked as if he was fighting his body's knee jerk reaction to drop to the floor.

Everyone fell silent before the sound of groaning metal echoed through the dining room. Sebastian snapped the towel bar off his serving cart. "We do not do that here," Sebastian said softly. He picked up a pair of serving tongs and stacked sandwiches on Pip's plate. "Let me know which ones you like best."

Pip turned to Meryn. "I cannot eat all of this," he confessed.

Meryn smiled. "I think that sometimes too, but then poof, it's so good I eat it all."

Pip picked up a sandwich with a trembling hand and bit into it. "So this is what fresh bread tastes like!" he exclaimed with child-like glee. Meryn handed him a soft roll and Pip hummed with sat-isfaction.

Another snapping sound came from Sebastian at his cart. This time, the serving tongs, bent in half, were the object of his frustration. Micah turned his head to hide his smile. He had a feeling Sebas-tian would be having a few choice words with the DeLaFontaine squire.

Bethy spun in her chair to face Gavriel. "You..."

He raised her hand and kissed it gently. "Consider this situation taken care of. Warrick requested a meeting after lunch and I have a feeling I know what it may be about." He inclined his head toward Pip.

Warrick grunted and nodded. Avery rubbed his mate's back soothingly.

"I've never in my life been more ashamed to call Noctem Falls my home," Bethy whispered.

Adriel covered her other hand with his. "We must trust in Fate. A lot of wonderful things have come about in our darkest hours of late."

"He is right," Pip agreed. "I did not know what would happen when father went to the detention cells. But now we have Warrick to help us on Level Five and he looks huge like he can protect us. And I got to meet Meryn who introduced me to soft bread!" Pip bounced excitedly.

Warrick smiled at the way Pip described him. "I will do my best."

Aiden pushed over his bowl of soup. "Try dipping it in the chicken noodle soup, then eating it."

Pip tentatively reached out his precious soft roll and dipped it into the soup. When he took a bite his eyes rolled back in his head. "It is like magic!" he whispered in a reverent tone.

Aiden scooted the bowl so that it was squarely in front of Pip. "You work on that one."

"You're a good man Aiden McKenzie," Rheia said smiling.

Aiden blushed and shrugged his shoulders. "It's just soup."

"Wait until you try Magic Pudding, then dinner, then coffee, then breakfast, then tomorrow's lunch, plus snacks!" Meryn exclaimed.

Pip turned to her. "There's more?"

She grinned. "You have no idea."

"Let's take it one meal at a time *denka*. That way he can be surprised and enjoy each new discovery," Ryuu suggested.

"Good point," she agreed.

"Maybe we should introduce everyone," Micah suggested.

"That's a wonderful idea," Ellie agreed. She held up Benji. "Hello Pip, my name is Benji, pleased to meet you," she said in a squeaky voice.

Pip giggled. "Hello Benji," he said waving. Ellie went up and down the table introducing everyone and explaining who they were and what they did.

As soon as she finished Pip stood and pointed to each person repeating each name and whatever information Ellie shared. When he was done he looked down to Meryn expectantly.

She beamed up at him. "You're not slow, you're a freaking genius. How'd you do that?"

Pip sat back down. "It is easy if I put the information away correctly." He frowned. "But sometimes I do not understand what people tell me, not like everyone else."

Avery gasped. "You're like me! It's called having a photographic memory. But I have a hard time understanding some social cues if they aren't explained to me."

Meryn nodded. "Yeah, they fuck me up too."

Pip looked down the table at Avery. "I am not broken?"

Avery shook his head emphatically. "No! In fact you're special." He turned to his sister. "I've learned that being different isn't such a bad thing after all."

Kari leaned over and kissed him on the top of his head. Meryn watched carefully then leaned over and kissed the top of Pip's head. Pip touched his hair a look of wonder on his face. "My first kiss."

Meryn smiled. "I thought it only counted if you got kissed on the lips."

Pip kept his hand on his head. "No. That is the first time anyone has ever kissed me."

"I am so going to fuck that douchebag up," Meryn whispered under her breath.

Rex cleared his throat. "I didn't hear anything."

Gavriel shrugged. "I have no idea what you are referring to."

Pip frowned and pointed to Meryn. "She said that..."

Aiden wrapped an arm around Pip and covered his mouth. He leaned in and in a clearly conspiratorial whisper said. "They know."

Pip blinked and Aiden removed his hand. "Oh!" he then shared an evil grin with Meryn. "I get it."

Meryn smiled back at Pip before she began to frown. She stood, then walked to stand between the twins' chairs. She kissed both of them on the head then returned to her seat. They exchanged the same poleaxed expression.

"Just in case," Meryn said reaching for a sandwich.

"Look at you! Amelia would be so proud," Rheia teased.

Meryn shrugged. "They're not so bad. They don't wrap themselves around me like an octopus the way Amelia does."

Micah knew in that moment that the twins

would walk through fire for the tiny human. He had a feeling Pip would be no different. He was about to ask what she meant when a loud alarm interrupted their lunch. All eyes turned to Meryn.

"What is that?" Gavriel asked.

"The front door alarm," Meryn explained.

"Front door?"

"Yeah, you know, the only door into the city. The big ass door. If that's not the front door, what is?"

"What does the alarm mean," Bethy asked.

Meryn tapped her lips. "Either someone is sneaking in, or someone is sneaking out."

"Well, which one is it?" Aiden growled.

Meryn shrugged. "No idea."

"How do we find out?" Micah asked.

"Go look," she advised.

Aiden and Adriel left at a run.

Meryn shook her head. "Seriously, I hafta think for everyone sometimes." She pulled out her laptop from the bag by her chair and opened it up. Everyone watched as the alarm blared.

With a few taps of her fingers the loud alarm stopped. She stared at her screen. "Well, it's someone coming into the city. Three someones. It looks like they are explaining things to Adriel." She closed her laptop.

"Adriel is leading them toward the tunnel so they are probably coming here."

Micah exchanged looks with Declan, Etain and Grant. "How in the hell did they get here?"

"We're about to find out," Meryn said grinning.

CHAPTER TWO

SERENITY FOLLOWED BEHIND THE HUGE Unit Commander. She felt like an idiot. Of course they hadn't been expecting them, they moved so quickly after the Witch Council meeting that Noctem Falls hadn't been notified. It was a miracle they hadn't been shot.

She was surprised when they floated down to Level One. From everything she read about the vampire city, Level One was known as the Royal Level. Queen Aleksandra told her that Prince Magnus had taken a personal interest in curing the virus, but she assumed that meant he publicly supported any medical efforts. Why were they here?

As they pass a hallway Aiden pointed. "The infirmary and labs are down that way, along with the meeting room the doctors have been using. Magnus spared no expense when ordering equipment. Before he got sick he was working around the clock in an effort to help the children." Aiden stopped and looked at them. "I have a deep respect for him as a leader," he said quietly before continuing past the tunnel.

Serenity exchanged looks with Laelia and Rad-clyffe. Aiden's quiet statement spoke volumes about the vampire prince. She was doubly glad she ignored the council to come. Men like Prince Magnus were rare, especially in leadership positions.

When Adriel opened the door without knocking, Serenity looked back at Radclyffe and Laelia. They both looked as surprised and nervous as she felt.

Adriel lifted his arm and pointed to the dining room. "Luckily you caught us at lunch time, so we will be able to get you up to speed."

When Serenity walked in she was shocked to see Kendrick Ashwood sitting at the table munching away on a sandwich. "Kendrick!" she exclaimed.

Kendrick looked up, inhaled and started to choke on his lunch. Aiden pointed and laughed. "Not so funny when it happens to you is it?" he teased as he sat down next to a dark-haired young man.

Kendrick stood pounding his chest. Scowling at her fiercely he walked over to them. "What on earth are you three doing here?" he demanded.

"We've come to help," Serenity said simply.

Kendrick looked from her to Radclyffe then to Laelia. He pinched the bridge of his nose before giving Laelia a sour look. "You couldn't stop them?"

Laelia smiled and stood on tiptoe to kiss his cheek. "We've missed you too." She looked around. "What's for lunch?" She glided easily past Kendrick to take an empty seat.

"Oh, I like her already," Rheia said. "Are you a nurse?"

Laelia laughed. "In a way, yes."

Kendrick exhaled and pointed to them. "This is Serenity Meadowsweet, the temple head for the Water Temple in Storm Keep. The two who should have hogtied her and kept her home are her best friends and water temple dedicates Radclyffe and Laelia Juniper."

Radclyffe clapped a hand on Kendrick's shoulder. "You're the only one who likes tying people up old man. Don't project that kink on to me and my mate." He walked past Kendrick to join Laelia at the table.

Kendrick rolled his eyes and pointed her to the table. "You might as well sit down."

She gave him a flat look. "Thanks ever so much," she said sarcastically taking the seat next to Radclyffe.

Kendrick sat down next to a woman who was trying to catch her breath from laughing. "Oh hush you," he said smiling.

"My name is Anne Ashwood, Kendrick's mate," the woman said introducing herself.

Kendrick looked around wincing. "We should do introductions again."

The dark-haired young man next to Aiden popped up out of his chair waving his hand. "Let me! Let me!" he begged.

Serenity was shocked at the gentle smile on Kendrick's face as he nodded to the youngster. He wasn't known for his patience in Storm Keep. In fact, she had heard many a witch create dares involving approaching Kendrick for a spell or advice. He was legendary for being grouchy and ill-tempered. Maybe being mated had mellowed him.

Starting with himself Pip introduced everyone giving her a bit of information with each introduction. When he introduced the warrior Micah Sageson, her heart began to race. How? How could this be the man from her dreams? Under the table she squeezed her hands together. Was he her mate? Or did she have a premonition about him warning of something terrible about to happen because of the sickness? Micah looked a bit shell shocked. Had he dreamt of her too? He recovered quickly and winked at her in a conspiratorial fashion. He threaded his hands behind his head and tilted back in the chair watching her closely.

She turned quickly to smile at the sweet youngster. "Thank you Pip, that was wonderful."

He beamed at her. "I just met them too."

Serenity stared. "You've memorized everyone's names that quickly?"

Pip nodded looking proud. "Meryn says I am a genius."

"I'll say," Laelia agreed.

Serenity smiled at the two other familiar faces. "Hello boys."

"Hey Seri!" they said waving.

She had a huge soft spot for Nigel and Neil Morninglory. Between helping to care for the other youngsters at the orphanage and training for their warrior exam, they spent a lot of time at the Water Temple. They seemed to be the only ones who could be around Kendrick without being blasted or turned into small animals. When they were assigned to Noctem Falls she found herself missing them terribly.

"Now that you know everyone. How did you get here?" Kendrick asked.

"Queen Aleksandra found the Healer's Clause in the original spell used to create the city portals. It states that if a portal is opened from within the Water Temple, witches are able to pass through to assist in any type of crisis. She pretty much got us up to speed on what's been happening here. I have to say, I am very impressed with the progress you've made thus far."

Kendrick rubbed his chin. "I'm surprised that the Witch's Council allowed you to come." Serenity winced and looked away. "Please tell me you didn't disobey the Witch's Council to come here?" Kendrick said in a low voice.

Serenity turned back and scowled at one of her oldest friends. Unlike other witches in Storm Keep his poor attitude hadn't affected her in the slightest. She simply ignored it. "Where the hell else would I be? The Water Temple has the largest collection of body magic spells on record. Ever since I took over as temple head I've incorporated healing magic into daily studies. You have yourself to thank for that, by the way. You were a huge influence on me growing up and as I reorganized the Water Temple."

Kendrick threw his arms up in frustration. "I wanted others to know how to heal so everyone would leave me alone, not for you to be prosecuted by those puffed up, self-important muppets."

"Muppets," Meryn repeated snickering.

"Maybe it won't be that bad," she said, not really believing her own words.

"She'll just have to stay here," Micah suggested

giving her a saucy wink.

"Leave the poor woman alone Micah," Kendrick groused.

"Never. She's my mate," he announced silencing the table.

Kendrick blinked. "She's what?"

"She's my one and only," Micah said meeting her eyes. There was a peacefulness about him that projected an almost a spiritual contentedness. The way he called her his one and only nearly brought tears to her eyes.

"It's about damn time!" Declan exclaimed pounding Micah on the back. "Congratulations to you both!"

Kendrick's perpetual scowl returned as he looked at her. "Is he right? I know that our mating dreams can be a bit tricky."

She gave a slow nod. "I've been dreaming of him. I just didn't know he'd be here."

"Micah Sageson... isn't he the horrible Lothario here in Noctem Falls?" Radclyffe asked glowering at Micah who blew kisses at him in return.

"Micah flirts all the time, but it's harmless. He's the sweetest guy ever," Meryn said. "He calls me his delicate flower and dewdrop," she added.

Meryn's proclamation had her heart sinking. Maybe her mate's endearment didn't mean anything to him. She felt silly for overreacting. She turned to Rheia and Ellie. "Put us where you need us. If we're going to get in trouble for coming I want to make a difference."

Ellie's eyes lit up in excitement. "What can you guys do to help?"

Laelia and Radclyffe exchanged smiles. Laelia

turned to Ellie. "Thanks to Serenity we've gotten so much better at healing. We won't be able to cure anyone, but we can bring down fevers, help with pain, and ease breathing. Our magic helps the body return to a healthy state."

Ellie and Rheia exhaled in relief. Ellie looked to them, tears in her eyes. "Thank goodness! Our medicines are losing their effectiveness by the day. I was terrified of what would happen when they were completely useless. The virus causes a lot of joint pain and I would've hated to see the children suffer."

Radclyffe draped an arm around the back of Laelia's chair. "We know absolutely nothing about science and human medicine, but we do know how to keep the body functioning. Our bodies want to work properly, so it's easy to help things along. It's nowhere near as taxing as trying to eliminate a sickness completely. As long as we have some time to recharge our magic and eat properly we can ensure that none of the children will be in any pain."

"Leave the healthy, filling meals to me," Sebastian promised.

"And leave finding a cure to me," Vivi said. She tapped her lips. "If you looked at a patient can you tell me if anything stands out as abnormal. For example higher white blood cell count or maybe inflammation?"

Laelia nodded slowly. "I would be able to point to a place on their body and tell you that they have an imbalance, but Serenity is better at the nitty gritty, like types of cells and chemicals released."

"She sounds amazing," Micah said his eyes still

locked on her.

She blushed and ducked her head. "After helping out the unit warriors so much I found that I had a knack for body magic. I tend to see a lot of illness and pain in the form of colors."

Her eyes strayed back to the pretty blonde sitting next to Prince Gavriel. She was torn. Did she know? Should she say something?

"Serenity, never play poker," Kendrick teased.

She looked up. "Huh?"

"Law and I saw it too. But I have to say I am very impressed with you. You saw it right away," Kendrick said pointing to Beth. "Do you know what it is?" he asked.

"Yes," she said nodding. She had noticed it immediately.

His mouth dropped. "What?"

Law burst into laughter. "Oh how the mighty have fallen! You've done nothing but scour your books and haven't got a clue!"

Gavriel leaned forward. "You know what the shadow is?"

Serenity hesitated. Kendrick frowned. "How bad?"

She winced. "Pretty bad." She took a deep breath. "It's a death curse."

Her words caused mass chaos around the table. Gavriel pulled Beth into his arms, Meryn began to shake, Beth's fathers moved closer to their child and Sebastian hurried over to stand behind Beth as if to ward off any harm. Micah stood and walked down the table to take the seat on her other side. Without saying a word he wrapped an arm around her.

She took a moment to appreciate his support. She had faced the world alone for so long that his small gesture meant everything.

Meryn looked at her, her lower lip trembling. "But, she's not dead right?"

Serenity smiled gently. "No Meryn, she's not dead." She looked at Beth again. "But not for lack of trying. I've never seen a more fragmented spell. It must have been trying to kill you for decades."

Beth stared at her stunned. "I think it has. I have the world's worst luck. I can't even begin to list the injuries I've sustained over the years."

"How in the devil do you know this?" Kendrick sputtered.

She raised an eyebrow. "Have you forgotten my heritage?"

Kendrick slumped back in his chair, eyes wide. "Of course!"

"What? What about her heritage. Can she fix Beth?" Gavriel demanded his worry making his tone harsh.

"Gavriel," Micah said simply. He stared at the prince a hard look on his face.

Beth placed both hands on her mate's chest. "Calm down my love. Kendrick already said this has been with me for a while, I'm not going anywhere."

Gavriel took a long shuddering breath. "My apologies Serenity, I did not mean to put you on the spot." He inclined his head to Micah. "Thank you for calling me out on it."

Serenity frowned. "That was shockingly humble of you, for being a prince."

Everyone around the table smiled at her observance. Micah turned to her. "He was a unit warrior first, we're a humble lot."

The women mostly shook their heads at that statement.

"Back to my mate...please," Gavriel insisted gently.

Serenity turned back to Beth. "I'm half fae, so I am extremely sensitive to black or dark magic. My magic is greatly affected by my fae blood. It's why I see things in colors, the way fae tend to see colorful auras. It's probably why I saw it right away and Kendrick didn't." She took a deep breath and reached deep into her magic. Suddenly the shadow around Beth became clearer and she was able to differentiate shades of grey and traces of bright colors. She let out a low whistle. "If I'm reading this correctly, it wasn't meant for you. It was meant for someone tied to you by blood." She winced. "Whoever cast this spell had a sick sense of humor."

"What do you mean?" Kendrick asked his brows knitted together.

She pointed to the darker grey color, even though she knew she was the only one who could see what she could. "The spell caster was simply that, the one that cast the spell. Another person wanted it done and the hatred they had for whoever this was intended for, is down-right frightening. What the spell caster didn't tell the person who requested the spell was that this particular piece of black magic required a human sacrifice." She glanced at Kendrick. "They killed the requester to cast the spell."

Kendrick blinked. "I see what you mean. Very tricky."

Serenity turned back to study Beth. When she

saw threads of amethyst running through the spell she began to piece together what may have happened. She looked at Broderick. "Were you and Beth's mother mates?"

He shook his head. "No, she wanted a child and I volunteered. We were both bunny shifters so it made sense." He inhaled sharply turning white as a sheet. "It was meant for me, wasn't it?"

She nodded. "I think so. The different shades of red are usually indicators of anger, hatred and jealousy. There's so much rage in this spell." She looked Beth in the eye. "But there's also a fierce thread of love, it's amethyst and beautiful." She smiled gently. "A mother's love and protection."

Beth's hands flew to her mouth. "My mother?"

"The carriage accident," Broderick said his voice trembling. "We were the ones who were supposed to go to town that day, but you weren't feeling well so I stayed behind to tend to you."

Serenity nodded absently as the story came together. "If the spell was affixed to the carriage to kill you Broderick, then when Beth's mother died instead, it followed the bloodline from her toward you because you shared a child together. But it reached Beth first since she was tied to both her mother and to you by blood."

"Oh gods, it's my fault," Broderick whispered.

"No, Papa it's not. It's whoever wanted this wickedness done who is at fault," Beth said hugging her father close.

"Who would want to kill Broderick and Beth that badly?" Caspian asked. "She was just a baby."

Serenity took another deep breath and refocused her magic. "Whoever it was had an extremely strong tie to Beth's mother."

"What if it was Beth's mom's mate?" Meryn suggested.

Broderick sat up straighter. "That could very well be it. Beth's mother said she was meeting someone in town, which is why she went in our place. She said she couldn't wait to introduce us. I didn't think anything of it after she died. Whoever he was must have seen us as a threat to their mating."

Serenity swayed a bit and Micah pulled her close. "There you have it," she said, shaking her head to clear the colors from her mind.

Gavriel blinked. "Have what? How do we get rid of it?"

Serenity shrugged. "We can't. It's so entrenched into her very aura there's no removing in." She smiled. "But on the bright side, it will dilute with each future generation."

Behind them they heard a loud thump. She and Micah turned in their chairs to look down. Micah turned back to the table. "Tarak fainted," he announced brightly.

"This is not funny Micah," Adriel admonished smiling wide.

"Gods no one tell Tarragon, he'll slit his own wrists," Declan muttered.

Gavriel stared down at the table eyes wide in shock. "Next generation?"

Broderick absently patted Gavriel on the back also looking a bit lost. "We can do it," he said nodding repeatedly in a daze.

"So. Jack will need a bubble huh?" Meryn asked.

Beth looked from her mate to her father to Meryn. She looked back behind them to the floor where Tarak still lay, out cold. "Don't call my baby Jack, Meryn." She smiled at everyone. "If my mother's love can protect me from a death curse, then I'm pretty sure I can keep my baby from getting hurt too badly."

Serenity gave her a short nod of encouragement. "Exactly."

"Oh I can't stand it," Radclyffe said standing. He walked over and placed a hand each on both Broderick and Gavriel's backs. He whispered low and after a few seconds both men sat a little straighter looking less stressed.

"Feeling better?" Radclyffe asked stepping back.

Gavriel looked up at the healer. "That was amazing. One second I could barely think and then it was like the fog cleared."

Radclyffe cracked his fingers. "Just negated a bit of shock is all." He walked back over to sit down next to his mate.

Broderick turned to Ellie. "They are exactly what we need, what the children need."

Meryn held up her hands forming a 'T'. "Okay peeps time out." She pinned Serenity with a questioning look. "So Beth is okay right? I just need clarification for that."

Serenity smiled. "Yes Meryn, she's just fine. She is as she always has been. In fact, from the gradient around the edges of the curse I would say she is better than she has always been. I think finding her mate and creating another bond helped to defuse the potency of the curse."

Gavriel sighed and sat back in his chair. "I would be too selfish to ask for more."

"I guess round two will not be too bad then," a

deep male voice said from the floor. Tarak stood shaking his head. He looked at Beth then rubbed the back of his neck. "The keystones will not work with an infant. Maybe a bespelled stone that would activate with certain pain levels," he turned and kept muttering to himself as he walked out of the dining room.

Gavriel looked exhausted as he smiled. "I like the way he thinks."

"Personally I think he's being overly dramatic," Beth sniffed raising her chin.

Around the table everyone fought to hide their laughter but soon everyone was chuckling out loud.

"Oh really!" Beth exclaimed.

Meryn looked over to Anne slyly. "If Anne hurries up and gets pregnant then her kid can heal your kid," she suggested.

Anne looked at Beth excitedly. "That's a great idea!"

Beth grinned back. "I forgot that my child won't be alone like I was growing up."

Serenity looked at Meryn. "What about your own child helping?"

Meryn thought about it for a moment. "I think my kid will be the reason why Beth's kid will get hurt to be honest." Everyone around the table nodded almost in sync with each other agreeing with Meryn.

Ellie stood. "I'm glad we know what that shadow thing is now." She stretched then turned to Laelia and Radclyffe. "If you all are ready, I can introduce you to the children and your other patients."

Serenity stood when her friends did. Laelia

turned to her and shook her head. "You spend some time with your mate. Radclyffe and I will run an assessment and update you during our next meeting." She looked around. "When would that be?"

"Dinner," everyone said almost immediately.

Radclyffe looked around. "Everyone eats here for every meal?"

Rheia nodded. "It ended up being easier that way."

Sebastian smiled. "With three squires here, it is actually quite easy to do. Feel free to leave your bags, I will move them to our guest quarters." He looked to Micah. "If it would make it easier, I can set up a room for you and your mate as well.

Micah smiled. "I think that may be a good idea, at least until the virus is cured."

Sebastian turned to Meryn. "And for Master Pip?"

Meryn frowned. "I hadn't thought through that far."

"He can stay with us in our house on the Unit Level," Nigel volunteered. "He's a vampire so he can just go back and forth between levels."

Pip gave a weak smile. "I am still a bit shaky when it comes to flying," he admitted softly.

Neil wrapped an arm around his thin shoulders. "No problem, we can help whenever you need us."

Pip looked up at him confused. "Why?"

Neil smiled at Meryn then looked down at Pip. "Because we're Meryn's brothers and you are too now, so we're going to look after you."

Pip nodded enthusiastically. "I think I am going to like having brothers and a sister."

Meryn shrugged. "It's not so bad."

Serenity raised an eyebrow to Kendrick who shook his head smiling. She thought that if anyone adopted the twins it would have been Kendrick. But from the boys' radiant expressions she knew they had finally found a place to call home, even if it was with a strange human.

Vivi turned to Serenity. "I don't wish to intrude on time with your mate, but before dinner, can you evaluate Prince Magnus? Our third treatment, as you know, is on hold until we can figure out what affected him so negatively. If you could give us half as many clues to work with as you did for Beth's curse, I feel like I would have a direction to move in."

Serenity glanced over to Micah who nodded. "Of course." Serenity smiled at him then turned back to Vivi. "I'll be back in a little bit to help with the prince."

Her words seemed to dismiss everyone as they all stood and began to leave the dining room.

Meryn held Pip's hand and led him past them. "Come on Pip, I get to show you my bat cave."

Pip frowned. "I do not like bats."

Meryn laughed. "You'll see."

Aiden followed behind them. "Don't overwhelm him Meryn," he chided.

Rheia looked at Serenity then winked. "They're all giant marshmallows I swear." She indicated to Pip. "I think Aiden will be more protective of him than Meryn will be." Serenity nodded smiling. She could already see that the huge commander had a protective streak a mile wide.

Laelia kissed her cheek. "See you soon," she promised and squeezed her hands encouragingly. Radclyffe just glared at Micah on the way out.

When they were the last two in the dining room she turned to her mate. "Hello," she said nervously.

Micah simply leaned forward until their foreheads were touching. "There are a lot of rumors about me, most of them aren't true," he whispered. "Just know that I have been waiting for you for a long time and I hope you try to get to know the real me."

When he stepped back his eyes held an element of vulnerability. Feeling daring she stepped into his body and rubbed their noses together. "I'm stubborn and tend to have to put my finger in the socket a few times to learn something, so if you have patience with me I will do everything I can to get to know my mate," she promised.

His face brightened when she used the term mate. "Deal." He took her hand and led the way out of the prince's quarter toward the transport tunnel. "Let's head to Level Six. You can meet some of the wolves and vendors, grab something to eat and even swing by the hospital before we check on Magnus."

Serenity felt a warmth expand in her chest. He noticed that she hadn't had a chance to eat and picked up on her impatience to see the children. "What about us?" she asked.

Micah smiled. "We have the rest of our lives my one and only. Until the threat to the children and prince are gone, I think I can share you." He paused. "Just a bit though," he said seriously.

"Thank you," she said simply.

"Let's go." He pulled her into the tunnel and together they floated up toward Level Six.

CHAPTER THREE

MICAH COULDN'T BELIEVE HIS MATE was walking at his side. Not only was she absolutely stunning with her dark brown curls and lavender eyes, her selflessness shined from her soul like a warm sun.

He led her by the hand until they found a table tucked away from the mid-day crowd. "You wait here, I'll grab my favorites for you to try," he suggested. She smiled up at him and nodded.

"Hey Micah, who is that with you?" Marcy asked as he approached her stall. She was one of his favorite vendors. Her specialty was sweet potato fries drizzled in brown sugar and cinnamon. "That beautiful soul is my one and only, my mate," he said proudly.

Around him voices died down. "You finally mated?" Old man Richter asked.

Micah grinned at him. "I sure am."

"Good for you boy. Tell your lady she is welcome here any time," he offered.

"Many thanks," Micah said waving.

Marcy had a shielded expression on her face as

she handed over his treat. She leaned in toward him. "Be careful with her Micah, you just broke a lot of hearts."

Micah frowned and looked around. He was shocked to see some of the ladies he knew dabbing at their eyes. He turned back to Marcy. "But they knew I wasn't their mate," he said taking his time reaching for the napkins.

"Which made your kind words all the more special." Marcy shook her head. "Give them a few days to adjust."

He winked at her. "You always take good care of me," he teased.

Even though she was old enough to be his grandmother she blushed before shooing him away. "Go on with you now."

Micah quickly grabbed some crepes and headed back to his mate. She eyed him suspiciously. "You seemed very chummy with that vendor."

He shrugged and sat down across from her. He handed her the sweet treats before murmuring a soundproof spell creating a bubble of privacy around them. "It's not easy being a female in Noctem Falls. It's getting better with Gavriel actively taking a huge role in setting things right. But before Aiden came to visit with his crazy mate and Bethy, the people here romanticized the Victorian Era, including how they sometimes treated women."

Serenity froze holding a fry in front of her. "You're joking right?"

He shook his head. "Everyone was very proper of course and publicly respectful, but I don't think many of the women here heard a kind word behind closed doors." He hummed as he chewed his fries. "So good! Anyway, when I first got here I would wink, flirt and compliment every woman I met. You could see it in their eyes that my silliness gave them just a moment of pride. A unit warrior had called them beautiful. They stood straighter or smiled more. Pretty soon I had a reputation for being a womanizer, but the ladies knew the truth. In all the years I've been here, I've never gone hungry or wanted for anything. Those same ladies would arrange for baskets of food to be delivered to the Unit Level or take in my wash if I was running behind on my home chores. Duties that they normally performed daily, but for the first time, it was something they wanted to do." He looked up at his mate. "I have many friends in the city and about ninety-five percent of them are female."

Serenity's eyes were filled with sympathy. "It's nothing like that in Storm Keep. Women are on a pretty level playing field with men. What matters more than gender are your test scores." She eyed him carefully. "Wait a minute, how are you still here?" She looked him up and down. "You must have tested extremely high."

"You can see my magic?" he asked curiously.

"Sort of. More like a range of color. Yours has amazing depth."

He shrugged. "Like most unit warriors I fudged my test scores so I could come back to the city after testing." He winced then looked at his mate. "And I sort of slept with the proctor's wife."

She started to choke on her crepe. She pounded on her chest before looking up at him. "You what?"

"They weren't mates," he said quickly. "I would

never, ever sleep with a mated woman. They had married at her parent's insistence to have more powerful children. I was a weekend delight."

Serenity leaned in. "Which proctor?" she asked her eyes dancing.

He waved a finger back and forth in front of her. "I don't kiss and tell, but needless to say he banished me from Storm Keep for a while."

She frowned. "I may be banished as well."

"Well, you're in good company."

She swirled one of her fries around her plate. "What would I do here Micah? After this virus is cured they won't have a need for a healer."

"Maybe they will. We don't know how long the wolves and kiddos will be here. Plus you could teach healing classes to unit witches, we could always use more healing knowledge amongst the units."

"Kendrick could do that," she started then shook her head. "Never mind."

Micah shuddered. "I respect that man more than any other witch I have met, but I would hate to sit a class with him. His suggestion to Aiden to teach us about childbirth was traumatizing." He shuddered remembering that awful video.

"Gods! He didn't!" Serenity exclaimed before dissolving into a fit of giggles.

Micah stared at her flatly. "It's not funny." His words only seemed to incense her more.

"I had nightmares."

She wrapped her arms around her stomach and toppled to one side on the bench. Her laughter was the only indication he had that she was still breathing.

"Then he had Sebastian serve a stuffed turkey for lunch," he continued.

When he heard a thump he looked under the table grinning. His prestigious mate was on the floor with tears streaming down her face. "Stop, I beg you," she managed to get out waving a hand at him.

He got up and walked around the table to help her up. She was laughing so hard she was practically limp. He held her up by her armpits as she calmed down.

When he looked around he noticed they were getting some strange looks. They must look ridiculous with the soundproof spell still going. He shrugged and the men just nodded their sympathy.

Finally, after a few minutes she took a few deep breaths wiping her eyes and cheeks with her napkin.

He leaned down and kissed her nose. The pure joy in her eyes filled his heart. "I am going to love you until the end of time," he promised softly.

Her mouth opened slightly when she inhaled and he took advantage of her distraction. He wanted to finally get a taste of his mate. He cupped the back of her head and took her lips between his own. He suckled on her plump lower lip groaning at the faint taste of cinnamon and sugar. When he pulled back her creamy cheeks were flushed pink, her lips were swollen and she looked throughly claimed.

Despite the growing problem in his pants he was proud of his work. He knew right then and there he would never get enough of her.

"Please don't break my heart, because I think I'm already falling in love with you," she whispered.

"There will never be anything else in this world I will cherish more than your heart, your love and your trust," he vowed.

He swaggered back over to his seat and sat down. Cursing, he jumped back up, took a deep breath and tried to covertly adjust his pants. Because he was no less affected than she was by their kiss he had almost gelded himself with the zipper.

She gave him a satisfied look. "Let those ladies see what I do to you," she said winking and jerking her head to one side pointing to their captive audience.

Wincing he shook one leg and gingerly sat down again. "Rub it for me later?" he asked leering at her.

She threw her head back and laughed. "Only if you kiss me like that again."

"I fully planned on it," he said in low voice.

When she shuddered at his deeper tone he picked up another fry. He'd have to figure out a way to cover his mate in cinnamon and sugar later. She was now his new favorite treat.

When they wrapped up their snack she stood on shaky legs. Her mate had a way of spinning her world around and making her feel like the most desired woman in the world.

As they walked toward the hospital she caught more than one hateful glare. After hearing her mate's explanation she decided to take a leap of faith. What he said made sense and if he was going to lie, she didn't think he'd confess to sleeping with the proctor's wife.

No, she truly believed her mate just had a heart of gold and enjoyed seeing those around him happy. So, she decided it was her job as his mate to make sure he was happy.

She eyed him carefully as they walked. It didn't look like making him happy would be that big of a chore. He was currently humming and swinging their hands back and forth between them. He was absolutely adorable and not afraid in the least bit to show his affection for her. His declaration earlier by the vendors stalls that he was mated went a long way to easing her fears. She sent up a small prayer of thanks that her mate wasn't a score obsessed bureaucratic suck up from Storm Keep.

When they walked into the hospital she noticed that Laelia and Radclyffe were off to one side with Ellie and Rheia. As they got closer she realized she couldn't hear anything. She waved her hands to get their attention. Radclyffe held up finger and lowered the soundproof spell. She and Micah stepped closer and Micah raised another one.

"What's going on?" she asked.

Ellie looked close to tears. "The antivirals and pain reducers we've been using are no longer working. Thank the gods you arrived when you did. I don't know what we would have done if the children got irate again." Grant massaged her shoulders lovingly.

"The queen did say that was an early symptom. Did it return?" Serenity asked.

Rheia nodded. "We saw last night that the children had a hard time falling asleep. They kept thrashing about complaining of pain. This afternoon they began lashing out at their parents again."

"We're running out of blood from the second batch and we're scared to try any older blood from the third treatment that turned Magnus violent," Vivi continued.

"Why don't we just get the guys to donate again?" Micah suggested. He knew his fellow unit brothers had no problems donating for the children.

"We're afraid that if we continue giving them what we're calling 'younger generation' blood, the virus will adapt and any chance we have at knocking it out completely with the older blood will disappear," Vivi explained looking pale. She ran a hand through her dark red hair. "We're missing something, I just don't know what it could be. We've talked every problem-solving scenario to death."

Marjoram wrapped an arm around Vivi. "Let's head down to the meeting room and go over things again. I've found that new people bring with them fresh perspectives." She nodded to Laelia, Radclyffe and Serenity. "Besides you need to get off your feet missy." Micah lowered the soundproof spell as Marjoram steered Vivi toward the exit.

"That's actually not a bad idea. I'm going to invite Meryn too. I don't know why she wasn't included from the beginning," Rheia added as they all followed behind Marjoram.

Serenity turned to the human doctor. "Does she have medical training?"

Rheia snorted. "Not a lick of it, but she thinks differently than we do. If anyone can help us figure things out, it would be our menace."

Anne chuckled. "I'll swing by her bat cave and the lab to pick up Meryn, Law and Kendrick. I'll meet you in the meeting room." She waved then jogged toward the tunnel before jumping down.

Serenity nearly stumbled turning to Rheia in a panic. "She's human!" she exclaimed.

Rheia laughed holding up a small stone. "The twins made these for us. Meryn calls them her floaty stones. They allow us to navigate the tunnels without waiting for an escort."

Serenity clutched at her chest. "I think I had a heart attack," she complained.

"Pull on your big girl panties because you're about to experience a brain storming session with someone who creates chaos as naturally as she breathes," Rheia looped her arm through Serenity's.

Serenity looked up at Micah feeling a bit out of her depth. He shrugged. "My delicate little flower is an experience all her own."

"What the hell have we gotten ourselves into," Radclyffe muttered.

"Sounds exciting," Laelia teased.

Serenity followed her colleagues to the tunnel wondering indeed what the afternoon had in store for them.

An hour later Serenity simply stared at the small human who kept spinning in circles in her chair.

Everyone around them ignored her and began the meeting, starting at the very beginning for their benefit.

Serenity sat next to her mate around a very impressive looking wooden conference table along with Rheia, Anne, Vivi, Ellie, Marjoram, Kendrick, Law, Laelia, and Radclyffe. Meryn's squire Ryuu stood quietly in the corner watching his charge a soft smile on his lips.

"She'll make herself sick," she warned.

Meryn stopped her spinning. "I do this all the time, it helps me think."

Radclyffe turned to Kendrick. "So, we know that DeLaFontaine is the one who distributed virus?"

Kendrick nodded. "We found a very intricate delivery system built into his cufflink. We can only hypothesize that he took advantage of both the welcome bar-b-que for the wolves and the fair to get to his victims."

Meryn began spinning again. "That may be wrong," she said to no one in particular.

Kendrick chuckled. "I did say it was a hypothesis Meryn. It does make sense he would use that opportunity to reach as many people as possible, the timing is right as well."

Meryn kicked out her foot halting her spinning. "That's not what I meant. DeLaDouchebag would poke people and they would get sick right? It's how Magnus got it."

Kendrick nodded. "Exactly. He used his cuff after dinner to infect Magnus."

Meryn tilted her head. "Then why isn't Aiden sick? He got nicked too."

Kendrick froze before turning to Ellie, who

looked Law who nodded. "She's right."

Vivi stood her hands shaking. "I need his blood!" she bolted from the room.

Meryn sighed, picked up her walkie-talkie and unclipped it from her backpack. "Work smarter not harder people." She pressed the button. "Boo-Bear, come in BooBear"

"Are you okay?" Aiden came back immediately.

"Yup I'm good. But can you meet Vivi in the lab she needs you."

"Sure thing. Love you."

"I lurves you too, catch ya later." She clipped her walkie-talkie back on her bag.

"I am really loving my call sign right now Meryn," Micah said grinning. Serenity raised an eyebrow. "Casanova," he replied.

"Of course, it is," Radclyffe said rolling his eyes.

"Serenity needs one," Meryn said tapping the table. She grinned at her. "You have the same name as my car."

Serenity eyed the small human. "Firefly or Sailor Moon?"

"Firefly," Meryn admitted. "Though, thanks to Anne I have a whole new appreciation for anime. One of the furries in my cult suggested something called *hentai*, I can't wait to Google it."

Ryuu stepped forward looking concerned. "I would not suggest that *denka*."

Meryn eyed her squire. "Why?"

"It's a lot of tentacle porn," Anne explained. When all eyes swung her way, she blushed and ducked her face into Kendrick's chest.

"Well, well, well," Kendrick murmured.

Anne popped up and flicked his ear. "Whatever

you're thinking, just no." He continued to grin as he rubbed his ear.

Serenity turned back to Meryn. "Wait. Furries? Cult?"

Rheia put her pen down and leaned back in her chair. "She means her shifter friends on Facebook and her Facebook group." She stood. "Okay, let's work under the assumption that Aiden was infected, what could be possible reasons why he's not sick?"

"Grant isn't sick either and he has every reason to be. He's been around the kids from day one and has been coated in just about every substance you can think of. He's fine," Ellie volunteered.

"Could it be because they're both Alpha Born?" Kendrick asked. "I haven't studied how their physiology differs from regular shifters."

Serenity spoke up. "I have. There were multiple volumes dedicated to Alpha Borns in the Water Temple. From what I've read, they are stronger and faster, but they are physiologically the same as any other shifter. Most changes seem to be metaphysical rather than scientific."

Rheia pursed her lips. "There goes that theory. We also have to keep in mind that none of the witches or fae are sick either."

Serenity shook her head. "Witches are more susceptible to sickness than the fae."

Meryn kicked off the table and started spinning again. "What if it isn't a race thing?" she asked.

Serenity just rolled with it. So far, this brilliant human gave the scientists the first break they had in weeks. "Keep going," she encouraged.

Meryn stopped. "This is Noctem Falls right?"

Everyone nodded. "The home of the vampires and mostly vampires. Like they are nowhere near as diverse as Lycaonia right?" Again, everyone nodded. "Aiden, the witches and the fae have another thing in common." She smiled at them. "In a city of vampires anyone who is fae or a witch is a unit warrior. None of the warriors are sick either and they've been helping from day one too."

Rheia gasped. "Oh my god! The reports! Adam's reports!" she screeched and ran from the room.

Meryn sighed. "I hate it when they do that. I wish they would share with the class before running out like a maniac."

Marjoram exchanged excited looks with Ellie. "We'll head back up to Level Six and work on keeping the children calm and comfortable. Let's leave the geniuses to work."

Anne, Laelia and Radclyffe stood. Laelia nodded to Marjoram. "We'll come with you. We couldn't help in a lab anyway." She turned to Serenity. "You go check up on Vivi and Rheia and keep us updated."

Meryn yawned then stood. "I'm heading back to my bat cave. I am introducing Pip to Magic Pudding and Doctor Who."

"If anyone deserves a reward today it's you Meryn," Marjoram praised. "Extra cookies for you later."

"Yes!" Meryn pumped her arm in the air.

"Come along *denka*, you can be amazing in your bat cave," Ryuu said steering his charge out the door.

Ellie and her helpers withdrew after Meryn leaving Serenity, Micah, Kendrick and Law in the meeting room.

Serenity shook her head. "She really is brilliant. How does she see things so simply?"

Kendrick frowned. "She said her grandmother used to tell her that her broken brain focused on the wrong things." He growled. "That hateful woman has had me seriously contemplating raising the dead, just so I could smack the shit out of her."

Serenity rolled her eyes. "You're always so dramatic."

Law watched their interaction with wide eyes. "She's not awed by your powers at all," he said sounding impressed.

Kendrick just grunted, and she beamed at him. "I love annoying him too much to be in awe of him," she admitted.

"Between you and the twins it's a miracle I got anything accomplished in the past hundred years," Kendrick said grumpily.

"Come on librarian, let's head to the lab to see what your elemental plates tell us about what type of magic is in the virus. The results should be in today," Law said standing.

"Archivist," Kendrick corrected.

"Why would you need..." Serenity started and saw the way Kendrick's eyes cut to her. "You know what, never mind. I'm more curious to discover what had Rheia running out of here like that."

Kendrick stood and bowed. "After you my lady."

"Thank you, kind sir," she said, walking past him.

Later she would ask why he was running tests to figure out which element was in the virus, because it had nothing to do with curing it, that could be accomplished regardless. She was still wondering what the grouchy witch was up to when Micah wrapped his arm around her waist. "We need to get you a call sign."

She smiled up at him sweetly. "How about Casa-novaKiller?"

"Serenity, one. Micah, zero." Kendrick said behind them.

Micah heaved a great sigh. "I am so abused," he said dramatically, placing the back of his hand to his forehead.

"You like it," she teased under her breath.

He opened his eyes and winked. "You'll find out later."

When they walked into the lab Vivi and Rheia were talking a mile a minute and Aiden's eyes looked glazed over.

Feeling sorry for the bear-shifter, Serenity caught Vivi's attention. "Do you need him anymore?" she asked pointing to the Unit Commander.

Vivi shook her head. "Nope, I already have his blood."

Serenity turned to Aiden. "You're free to go."

"Thank the gods! Call me if you need me again," he said quickly and before she could blink he was shutting the door behind him.

Over the walkie-talkie Ryuu's voice came through. "If possible, could Law relieve Etain guarding Meryn? Etain has been called to the hospital."

Kendrick picked up his walkie-talkie as Law left. "He's on his way."

"Many thanks," was the squire's polite reply.

Vivi was mid-sentence talking with Rheia when she stopped. "Why was Etain called to the hospital?"

"Oh, that. Ellie has been asking the fae warriors to rotate shifts at the hospital. They can easily lift the children, as well as the adults for sheet changes. It makes keeping the patients comfortable so much easier," Rheia explained.

Vivi blinked. "That makes sense. I'm really the worst person when it comes to nursing. Give me a microscope and slides any day."

"Speaking of slides, what had you running out of the meeting with your hair on fire?" Serenity asked Rheia.

Rheia blushed. "It's what Meryn said about the warriors not getting sick. Normally I would say it's because they are paranormals and paranormals don't get sick right?" She waved her hand about. "Except we now know they can get sick. We have shifters and vampires ill up on Level Six, but not the warriors."

"What does that tell us? How are they different?" Serenity asked thoroughly confused.

Rheia grinned wickedly. "Last year our menace conned the public works of Lycaonia into completely updating our clinic. But the downside to that was that they started asking for weekly reports on what was being done, kinda checking to make sure the money was well spent. Well, short of having the warriors break each other's bones on a weekly basis, which would have gotten really old, really fast, I suggested we give all the guys physicals."

Micah nodded. "Doc St. John did those here too. He said the warriors' care had to be uniform across all four pillar cities."

Rheia clapped her hands excitedly. "Exactly! The physicals included inoculations getting everyone an updated shot record!"

Serenity felt around for a stool and sat down. "One of the vaccines made them immune?"

Rheia and Vivi nodded enthusiastically. Vivi held up a slide. "That's what we're hoping anyway. If we're right it will take some time to isolate which one it is, but we finally have a direction to go in."

Vivi turned to Rheia. "I want to apologize. When you first suggested Meryn I was skeptical about what she could contribute, I thought she would distract us. But she really came through."

Rheia gave a smug smile. "Our menace is amazing."

Kendrick nodded. "That she is."

As Vivi and Rheia entrenched themselves with the new testing Serenity made her way over to Kendrick. She looked over to Micah and made a circle with her finger. When her mate was done casting the soundproof spell she leveled her gaze to Kendrick.

"Do you want to tell me why you're testing for elemental presence when it has nothing to do with a cure?"

CHAPTER FOUR

KENDRICK SIGHED. "I SHOULD HAVE known you'd pick up on that." He pointed to his table. It was evident from the multi-colored plates that he was testing for elemental influences. "Technically, finding out the elemental magic used in the virus can help. I have deduced that there is a sort of self-destructive command encoded within the virus. Once it drops below body temperature it erases any traces of the virus and magic within seventy-two hours, give or take."

Serenity nodded. "So by isolating the elemental magic used, you can nullify the magic giving Vivi more time to study the virus."

Kendrick nodded. "Exactly."

Serenity stared. "And?" He gave her a devilish grin. "*And*, if I can figure out which element was used I can begin tracing the magic back to the witch." He eyed the table. "There are very few witches in the world who can create something this intricate. I mean, you're talking about magic on a molecular level." He shrugged. "*I* can do it, but that's not really saying much."

"Kendrick..." Serenity growled impatiently.

Kendrick blinked. "Right. Anyway. There are only a handful of witches it could be, and I know all of them. If I can determine who it is, I can take the steps needed to ensure that this virus or any other like it never happens again."

Micah frowned. "But by creating this virus and infecting people, killing people, wouldn't the witch who created the virus turn feral and lose their magic?"

Kendrick shrugged slowly. "Welcome to Magical Ethics 101."

Serenity groaned. "It falls into a grey area doesn't it?" When she was studying for her exams she and Kendrick had gone round, for round discussing magical ethics. He always played devil's advocate and she usually ended up screaming at him. His favorite arguments took full advantage of what he liked to call 'grey areas'. Scenarios that were neither right nor wrong. Neither white magic nor black magic. Neither overtly helpful nor harmful. Just a vast, bleak, grey zone where some good was done, but mostly bad.

Kendrick nodded. "*Technically*, the virus in and of itself is harmless. The witch who created it didn't infect anyone." He held up a finger. "Now here's where it gets even trickier. DeLaFontaine is the one who distributed it, yet he's not feral. Why?"

Micah closed his eyes and shook his head. "Because he wasn't the one who created the virus." He opened his eyes to stare at Kendrick. "That's one of the most brilliant loopholes I've ever seen." He paused before continuing. "Who in the hell is behind this?"

Serenity stared down at the table. What Kendrick was doing made a lot more sense. If they could figure out the witch, they could use them to trace this back to whoever was pulling the strings. She glanced back to Kendrick. "Whoever is behind this used one of the oldest Founding Family heads as a pack mule," she whispered.

Kendrick nodded. "I knew you'd see the depth of this issue quickly."

"They must have solid brass balls," Micah murmured.

Serenity rolled her eyes. "What makes you think a man is smart enough to do this?"

"Hey," Kendrick and Micah protested.

She grinned. "Just saying." She walked over to the table. "Earth magic huh?" she said pointing down to the bright green tray.

Kendrick nodded. "I can use the twins to stabilize the magic in the virus, this should also help make it more visible."

"The boys?" she asked feeling anxious. She didn't want them anywhere near this magic.

Kendrick patted her shoulder. "They are grown now Serenity, you can cut the apron strings." He chuckled. "Besides, they rival me for earth magic power."

"Their test scores were barely passing," Serenity argued. There was no way Nigel and Neil had the same amount of power as Kendrick.

Kendrick rubbed the back of his neck while Micah chuckled. "I may have taught them how to hide their magic for the exams," he confessed.

Serenity looked to her mate. "You said something similar, about fudging your test scores."

Micah nodded. "Most witches who want to continue to serve as unit warriors have to hide their abilities to get lower scores or they would be contracted out by Storm Keep to earn money for the city. If you have mediocre scores they allow you to remain a warrior since the city is obligated to provide warriors for the units. It's why Leif and Travis were hiding out in Vegas. They accidentally displayed their magic when they prevented that mudslide while visiting home a while ago. The test administrators wouldn't have been fooled. Magnus did everyone a huge favor getting them reassigned back to Noctem Falls and their tests cancelled."

Serenity clenched her teeth in frustration. Instantly Micah was wrapping an arm around her and pulling her close. "What's wrong? What's upset you?"

She looked up at him tears in her eyes. "They barely even tested me because I'm not a full blooded witch. 'Half-breeds' are assessed at two-hundred and fifty years old instead of five hundred years old like full blooded witches. I had half the amount of time to study. They gave me the score they thought I should have. At the time, I fought for every point thinking I had a chance at working for the council, but after I received my score I was informed that although I had potential they were reserving those open positions for other candidates, in other words, you need not apply."

Kendrick nodded sympathetically. "I never did put much faith in their scoring system."

Micah rubbed her back soothingly. "Look at this way love, Kendrick's been sabotaging the system for centuries, that shitty score they gave you is meaningless." As the words tumbled out of his mouth they turned to each other, then to Kendrick who began to whistle and stare up at the ceiling as if he weren't single-handedly responsible for ruining an entire social structure.

Micah chuckled and Serenity wiped her eyes. "In a way I'm glad they turned me down. They initially asked me to act as a low-level secretary in the Magical Academy. I was stubborn and deliberately moved to the Lower City to take the position as the Water Temple head." She exhaled. "Thank the gods for whoever insisted on keeping the temple there, otherwise a lot people would have been denied care. Since it's in the Lower City the temple was hard pressed to fill positions. The placement board thought it was an appropriate assignment for me." She smiled. "It allowed me to help so many people and made my life so full that I can't imagine working in the Magical Academy, even if it is in a nicer part of the city."

"You've done a lot of good work, you should be proud," Kendrick said giving her a rare compliment.

"I get to work with Laelia and Radclyffe and I was able to help the boys," she listed.

"Speaking of the boys," Kendrick looked to Micah who took down the soundproof spell. Kendrick picked up his walkie-talkie from the table. "Frick, Frack, report to the lab as soon as possible."

"On our way," one of the twins responded.

Kendrick put the walkie-talkie down. "I can never tell them apart over these things."

Serenity smiled. "That was Neil. He usually takes charge and speaks up more than Nigel."

"Of course, you would know," Kendrick said putting his hands on his hips then leaning back to crack his spine.

"We'll leave you to it then," Serenity said before looking up at Micah. "I'd like to go check on Prince Magnus now."

"I can take you," Vivi volunteered. "Rheia can test the vaccine against the pure strain of the virus we got from DeLaFontaine. I'm praying we'll get a reaction we can see."

"I'll be able to help with that." Kendrick said. "My testing is done. We've figured out that it's earth magic in the virus. Now that we know the element, I'm going to have the twins help me stabilize the magic which should prevent it from wiping itself out and make it visible."

Vivi practically sagged in relief. "Thank the gods," she murmured reverently.

As they were leaving the twins were jogging up to the door. They both dropped a kiss on her cheek before going to meet with Kendrick.

"They are good boys," Vivi said once they were heading toward the prince's quarters.

"That they are, despite their rough start in life. You have no idea how much it means to me to see them so happy." Serenity felt like calling the Magical Academy gloating that the three of them found a place where they belonged, even with low test scores.

Vivi opened the door and walked in the same way that Adriel had. "You don't knock?" she asked.

Vivi shrugged. "We're kinda beyond knocking at this point. Why pull Sebastian away from whatever he's doing?"

"I appreciate that more that you know," Sebastian said walking in from the dining room wiping his hands on a towel.

"We're about to check on Magnus," Vivi said.

Vivi looked around. "Where's Meryn?"

Sebastian chuckled then coughed into his hand to hide his mirth. "Since the twins had to report to Kendrick in the lab, Master Pip decided to go visit Master Avery in the office. That left Meryn alone to keep Magnus company."

"Oh gods," Vivi whispered, then began walking down the hall.

Serenity and Micah followed. As they approached they noticed the door to the master suite was open and they could hear loud hissing and thrashing.

"Go ahead and try to bite me one more time Hissy. Remember Beth likes you, I have no problems punching you in the balls to get you to simmer down." Meryn's voice was clearly audible. Vivi covered her face with her palm.

Surprisingly enough the hissing softened. "There. Now Rheia says I have to have eight hours of quiet time or she'll shove a feeding tube down my nose. So, I am going to share one of my favorite relaxing TV shows with you. Okay Ryuu, press play."

"Of course, *denka*," Ryuu replied.

A soft soothing voice started speaking. Serenity frowned. "Are they watching Bob Ross?" she whispered.

"Happy little stormtroopers," Meryn said.

Micah nodded. "Yup."

Vivi walked through the doorway and they followed. Sure enough. Meryn had propped the prince of the vampires up in bed and was lying down beside him while Bob Ross played in the background. When Magnus saw them, he sat up and bared his fangs. Meryn raised a hand over his crotch and Magnus laid back down growling lowly.

Sebastian watched the entire scene looking like a proud father. "Only Meryn has been able to handle him."

Vivi shook her head. "I wonder why." She turned to her. "Do you need to touch him for this to work?"

Serenity shook her head. "No, I just need to see him."

"Do I need to get up?" Meryn asked plaintively.

"No Meryn, you're fine. Just try not to move around."

"Okie dokie," Meryn yawned and closed her eyes.

Serenity took a deep breath and called on her magic. Instantly her eyes were drawn up to the brain. Flashes of purple ignited in clusters. His testosterone levels were off the charts. She had never in her entire career seen anyone with levels that high and she had treated unit warriors after battle.

"Vivi, what exactly was in the treatment you gave him. The exact components," Serenity asked, keeping her eyes focused on Magnus.

"We used an older vampire's blood then mixed it with Caspian's to ensure compatibility and to prevent any type of bonding," Vivi explained.

"You're telling me the only thing he received was two strains of vampire blood?" Serenity asked.

"Yes."

"Who was the other donor?"

Vivi hesitated.

Serenity could understand the reluctance to share names, but in order to help Magnus she needed to know. "I'm not asking to be nosy and I am bound like any other physician to confidentiality. What you tell me, stays with me," she promised.

"You might as well tell her," Sebastian said. "It is bound to come up in conversation later anyway."

"It was Gavriel's blood," Vivi answered.

"Hmmm." Serenity continued to watch the lights flash in his brain. To her it looked like the Fourth of July. No wonder he was restless. His brain was sending mixed signals to his body.

"Hmmm? What?" Vivi asked.

"You said older vampire, right? Magnus is pretty old, can I assume Gavriel donated because he's older?"

"Yes, much older. In fact, he's probably twice Magnus' age."

Serenity blinked and turned away from Magnus to look at Vivi. "Really?"

Vivi nodded. "Gavriel is our Dark Prince, the son of one of our Originators. He's over ten thousand years old. We thought his blood was the answer, but then this happened," she pointed to the restraints.

Serenity looked around the room. "Does anyone have a walkie-talkie?"

Meryn pointed to Ryuu. "He has mine." Ryuu held it up.

"Could you call Gavriel down here please?"

"Of course," he said and lifted the walkie-talkie. "Gavriel could you report to the Rioux quarters please."

Meryn scowled. "You never use the call signs," she muttered. Ryuu winked at his charge.

"On my way," Gavriel replied.

Meryn giggled. "I bet he thinks it's Beth. He'll be here in two seconds flat."

"You would be right," a deep voice said from behind them.

Serenity stared. "How fast are you?" Her eyes narrowed. "Or were you just close by?"

Gavriel raised an eyebrow. "Is that what you called me down to ask me?"

"No. I'm trying to help Magnus. I was told you donated the blood for his treatment."

He inclined his head. "I did."

"Are you helping uncle?" Beth asked, walking into the room. Immediately Gavriel pulled her close to his body. She gave Serenity a lop-sided smile. "I didn't mean to interrupt but I heard Gavriel getting paged and came down." Serenity could see the wealth of love Beth had for her uncle. It had nothing to do with him being a prince. From the way she smoothed her hand over the sheets Serenity could tell that Prince Magnus was adored by his niece.

"You're not interrupting at all, I'm just assembling some facts so I can try to help." She turned back to Gavriel. "I know this can be a personal question for vampires, but I assure you, it is relevant. Have you recently gone through transition?"

Gavriel blinked. "As a matter of fact I have." He tilted his head. "How could you possibly know that?"

Serenity smiled as the final pieces of the puzzle fell into place. "I think I know what's wrong with him."

"You do?" multiple voices asked incredulously.

"It's an educated guess mind you, but..." Serenity walked over to the bed. "Meryn, could you pop up for a minute?" she asked reaching down to help the pregnant human stand. Meryn waddled over to her squire.

Immediately Magnus began to thrash about and hiss up at her. She ignored him and placed a hand on his forehead. She slowly sent her magic into his body. As she worked he became less agitated. She took her time making sure everything that could be returned to normal levels was. Once his chemistry was balanced she withdrew her magic and stepped back. Micah placed a hand on the small of her back and she could feel his magic seeping into her. He replenished what she expended, alleviating some of the fatigue. She looked up at him gratefully and he kissed her nose again. The man seemed obsessed with her nose.

When she looked around the room everyone was staring at Magnus who was sleeping peacefully a faint smile on his lips.

Beth turned to her, hope a living thing in her eyes. "What did you do? Is he okay?"

"I'm sure Vivi would have caught it eventually, but you all have been stretched so thin with the virus."

"Caught what?" Vivi asked.

"His testosterone levels were out of control," she pointed to Gavriel. "I think it's because he was reacting to Gavriel's blood which was still amped up from transition. Something in the virus reacted to those transition markers triggering aggression."

Sebastian gasped. "He was not feral, he was going through a transition?"

Serenity nodded. "Gavriel's blood triggered one. His body was caught in a loop. His transition was stuck due to the 'fight or flight' mode his body was in from the aggression triggers from the virus. Once I toned down the testosterone levels his transition ended."

"What about the virus?" Beth asked anxiously.

Serenity grinned. "Completely burned off."

Beth burst into tears at the news causing her mate to cuddle her closer. Sebastian was dabbing at his eyes with his tea towel as he walked over to Serenity. Without warning he pulled her into a warm hug. "Thank you!" he whispered, emotion making his voice harsh. He stepped back then hurried over to comfort Beth.

Serenity shrugged. "I feel like I'm getting all the credit when I just helped with the final steps. Vivi is the real hero."

Sebastian shook his head. "You brought him back to us, thank you," he repeated.

Meryn looked down at Magnus nervously. "Do y'all remember stuff from when you're raging from transition?"

Gavriel eyed her closely. "Why?"

Meryn was instantly a figure of innocence. "No reason."

Serenity looked over at the prince. "I'd leave him strapped down just in case, but he should wake up completely himself." She looked over to Sebastian. "He will need a lot of fresh blood, his body is nearly depleted."

Sebastian nodded. "Of course. It was just so hard trying to get him to feed when he was being..."

"Hissy," Meryn volunteered.

Sebastian winked at her. "Yes, hissy." He headed toward the door. "I will get a feast ready for tonight's dinner in your honor and to celebrate Magnus returning to us! Hal! Oh Hal! I need help in the kitchen!" Sebastian called down the hallway.

Gavriel eased Beth into the chair by Magnus' bed. She was wiping her eyes. "Stupid pregnancy hormones," she complained.

Serenity looked down at Beth's belly. "Your daughter is sleeping at the moment, so you can't blame her."

Gavriel looked up at her then down to stare at Beth's nearly flat stomach. When he looked back up he had tears streaming down his cheeks. "We have a daughter?"

Serenity nodded. "I checked earlier when going over her curse. She is doing just fine, perfectly healthy."

Gavriel wrapped his arms around his mate and buried his face in her shoulder. Beth held him close. When she looked up at them she was smiling broadly. "Thank you for this day."

Meryn sniffled. "Okay, so not Jack." She tapped her lips with her finger. "What about Jackie or Jacquelyn?"

Beth shook her head laughing. "No, Meryn."

Meryn shrugged and turned to Serenity pointing down at her belly. "Do me."

Serenity shook her head. "I've been trying, but your baby is turned in such a way I can't tell. But I can tell you this, they are very happy. I've never seen a baby radiate such happiness. They know they are loved."

Meryn blushed and stared down at the floor. "It's

probably the Magic Pudding," she said quietly.

Ryuu placed his hands on her shoulders. "Come along *denka*, you still need your quiet time, especially if you want to be rested for tonight's feast."

Meryn brightened. "Oh yeah! Tons of squire food."

Ryuu rolled his eyes as he steered her out of the room. "Yes, because you're so deprived of squire food," he teased.

Serenity took Micah's hand. "We'll give you some privacy." They were about to turn toward the door when she found herself in Gavriel's arms. When he stepped back his eyes were still bright but the tears had been wiped away. "Thank you," he said simply.

"It's why I'm here," she answered.

She walked hand in hand out of the room with her mate leaving Gavriel and Beth alone to discuss their daughter.

Once outside by the transport tunnel Micah turned to her. "Where to next boss?"

Serenity pulled out her phone from her pocket and checked the time. "When will dinner be?"

"Usually we meet up for drinks in the antechamber around six, then dinner is at seven. We go around the table and everyone reports in. We get our medical updates from the doctors. Unit updates from Adriel and Aiden. City updates from Gavriel, Kari and Beth. And the rest of us just fill in anything pertinent."

"So, we have a couple hours then." She put her phone away. "How about we check on the children?" she suggested.

Micah smiled. "You're on a roll. It wouldn't surprise me if you cure everyone by dinnertime."

She blushed. "If they are cured any time soon it will be because of the tireless efforts of Rheia, Vivi and Ellie. Those three are truly miracle workers. Working with so little they've managed to not only treat a growing patient load, but also figure out a partial cure. They've used human ingenuity and science, which to me is amazing. I feel like I fall back on to my magic too quickly. I'm hoping to learn as much as I can from them while I'm here. I bet Laelia and Radclyffe will feel the same way."

"I'm just teasing. Trust me, I know how much these ladies have done. But you really should get used to the gratitude and the compliments, if Magnus is able to join us tonight everyone will be singing your praises," he said as they stepped into the tunnel.

"Why?" she asked feeling confused. She really hadn't done much, just lowered his testosterone levels and ended his stalled transition.

When they stepped onto Level Six he placed a hand on each shoulder and turned her to face him. "Because you didn't have to come. In fact, coming here could cost you your position. But that didn't stop you. You may feel like you've only done small things, but those small things are tipping the odds in our favor. Even if what you do gives us a slight edge, that tiny advantage could mean the difference between celebratory dinners and another tragic funeral."

"Well said Micah," a male voice commented.

They turned to see Adriel beaming at them. He walked up to Serenity and hugged her. When he stepped back his mate took his place giving her another embrace.

Eva's smile was contagious. "Meryn texted us what happened. We understand a general announcement can't go out yet, but those of us who have been living out of Level One, fighting this day in and day out know what you've done. Everyone who received an update is walking around grinning like an idiot."

Serenity smiled feeling a bit like a fraud. "I keep telling Micah I didn't do much."

"And as my wise unit brother already told you, what you have done, no matter how small, has giant ramifications," Adriel reminded her.

Serenity threw up her hands. "Fine! You're welcome," she said laughing.

Eva bumped hips with her. "That's the spirit."

Adriel turned to Micah. "Have you considered my offer?"

Micah nodded then pointed to her. "I have, but need to run it by my mate before I can give you a final answer."

Adriel smiled. "As you should." He turned to Serenity. "Are you checking on the children?"

"Yes, and my dedicates. They have a tendency to go overboard with their magic if I don't keep them in line."

Eva turned to look back at the hospital. "Those two have worked miracles today. I haven't seen the children feeling so good since that first infusion of warrior blood."

Serenity couldn't help feeling proud. She knew how hard both Laelia and Radclyffe studied so they would be able to help others. "They are two of the most selfless people I know."

"We will not keep you from them any longer." Adriel said looping his arm around his mate. "Do not forget to speak with Serenity about my offer."

Micah nodded. "See you at dinner." Adriel and Eva waved then dropped out of sight.

Serenity turned to Micah. "Should I be worried?"

He gave her a boyish grin. "Nope, it's actually a really cool offer. One I don't think we'll turn down. But we can discuss it later when we're alone."

CHAPTER FIVE

WHEN THEY ENTERED THE HOSPITAL Serenity found Laelia and Radclyffe each visiting different children. The girl Laelia was with was showing her a stuffed animal that looked like a weird chicken and Radclyffe was reading a story to an enthralled audience. Serenity shook her head at his antics. He was completely going overboard using his magic to do sound effects, but she supposed the result was worth it. He was entertaining everyone around him.

She decided to let them continue their visits as she walked to the center of the floor. She sent her magic out to everyone in the room. She didn't limit herself to just the patients, she also reached out to the parents, the warriors, the helpers, to Ellie and Anne and especially to her two best friends.

She reduced anxiety, upped endorphin and serotonin levels, eased pain, and generally sent out waves of happiness and love. When she opened her eyes, everyone was staring at her, soft smiles on their faces. "There, I think I earned an extra helping of dessert tonight," she said, winking at the children. They laughed, and their parents laughed with them. She concentrated most of her efforts on the exhausted figures watching over their children. When she walked in the mothers and fathers looked worn down, scared, and hopeless. She knew that children, especially, picked up on ambient moods. She hoped by giving the caretakers a pick-me-up it would in turn help the children relax for the evening.

Laelia walked over and kissed her cheek. "We're still learning from you. Thanks for noticing what we missed."

Serenity kissed her friend's cheek in return. "I was only able to help because you and Radclyffe did such an amazing job with the children. I had to find something to do," she teased.

Radclyffe waved to the kids he had been reading to and jogged over. "Marjoram said we could stay with her on this level instead of on Level One. We'll be closer to the children and it will be easier to do rounds."

Marjoram, Ellie and Anne joined their group. "I'll be grateful for the company. Ellie, Grant and Benji moved in with his unit on Level One."

Serenity looked at Micah. "Is it normal for warriors to live on the royal level?" she asked.

He shook his head. "That was the decision I was going to talk to you about later."

Serenity looked from Laelia to Radclyffe. "What about your things?"

Marjoram smiled. "I already used that handy walkie-talkie the warriors carry. Sebastian sent their things up earlier."

Marjoram leaned down and kissed Serenity on

the cheek. "I heard what you were able to do. Thank you. Looks like both you and Meryn will be getting extra cookies."

Micah leaned forward. "Cookies?"

Marjoram pointed to Serenity. "See if your mate is willing to share."

Micah turned to her with such a pitiful expression she couldn't help but laugh. "Of course I'll share my cookies with you. You introduced me to your favorite treats on Level Six."

"Yes!" Micah exclaimed enthusiastically.

Ellie giggled. "Grant is the same way when it comes to Marjoram's cookies."

Serenity found that hard to believe. She couldn't imagine the stoic warrior acting like her light-hearted mate one bit. "They must truly be amazing," she said.

Ellie sighed happily. "They are."

Radclyffe turned to his mate. "You ready to go? We have some time to wind down before dinner on the royal level."

Serenity frowned. "We're really eating on Level One?" she asked, feeling a moment of panic.

They nodded their heads. "We weren't expecting to hobnob with royalty and Founding Family members, but Ellie has assured us we're welcome. Honestly we'd be perfectly content to eat home-made lasagna with the twins and their friends on the Unit Level."

Serenity looked at Micah. "Who're the royalty and Founding Family members who will be at dinner?"

Everyone just stared at her. Laelia finally took pity on her confused state. "Weren't you paying attention to the introductions earlier?"

Serenity nodded, then shook her head. "I heard names, but I was too busy wondering what Kendrick was doing here and staring at Beth." She looked around. "I think I would have remembered if someone introduced royalty though."

Marjoram smiled. "I think I see the problem. She knows everyone's names but not their rank. I can see where she would be confused, everyone is so casual on Level One that you kinda forget they are important. It's almost like they're *real* people," she said in a playful mocking tone.

"Gram!" Ellie admonished blushing.

"Wait, so who's important?" Serenity asked.

Micah rubbed the back of his neck. "It would be easier to list those not holding rank."

"Surely not Meryn," Serenity said jokingly.

Micah nodded. "Mate to the Unit Commander and future Lady McKenzie of House McKenzie. She was adopted by Beth as a sister tying her to House Rioux and House Ambrosios. Her cousin is mated to Darian Vi'Alina who was raised by Queen Aleksandra of the fae and she's the newest owner of the Gown of Eiré Danu," Micah listed.

"That amazing little oddball?" Serenity whispered. Everyone nodded.

Laelia turned to Micah. "Maybe you should take Serenity somewhere to unwind as well. You could also go over the guest list so she doesn't have a panic attack at dinner."

Serenity was frowning down at the floor. "I mean I knew about Prince Magnus and Prince Gavriel, they exude power, but Meryn just exudes geek references and *Cheeto* powder."

Micah physically turned her to face the door. "We'll see you all later." He gave her a gentle push towards the exit.

"She's just so..." Serenity continued looking over at her mate.

He grinned wickedly. "Yeah, she is."

Micah decided the best place to take her was his home on the Unit Level. When they stopped in front of his home he suddenly felt inadequate. If you compared his medium sized English style cottage to Declan's castle or Etain's fae treehouse, his home looked dowdy.

"I love it," his mate whispered staring up at the house.

"You do?"

"I've always loved homey places," she admitted an infectious smile on her face.

"Welcome to my most humble abode," he said with great flourish.

They stepped onto the stone path and his mate gasped. Oh, yeah. He'd forgotten about the house-warming spell he put in the stones. Seconds later his mate was on her knees her hands spread out over the odd shaped grey stones. "What spell is this?" she asked

"Ever the scholar." He knelt beside her. "There are three spells woven into the stones. Welcoming, laughter and safety. To me that makes a place to call home."

She gently ran her hand over the small pink and purple flowers growing between the stones. "Is that Mother of Thyme?"

He nodded quietly. "I dug some up from my grandmother's garden in Storm Keep and brought it with me." She slowly crushed the plant to release the aromatic fragrance. She smiled up at him. "I could spend the entire day on your walkway and be perfectly happy."

He helped her to stand. "Then you'd miss what's on the inside."

As they walked up to the door he saw that Ms. Anderson had left his basket of wash by the door. "Gods bless that woman." He smiled sheepishly at his mate. "I can perform just about any major spell I attempt but for some damn reason every time I wash my clothes they either turn pink, blue or grey."

Serenity instead of laughing nodded in sympathy. "Do you think she'd be willing to take on my wash too? I'd be more than happy to pay her for the trouble. I hate doing laundry," she admitted.

"I knew we were meant for each other." Micah leaned down and kissed her soundly. What started out as an impulsive kiss of joy turned heated quickly. When she began to pull him close he stepped back. He placed a trembling hand on the center of the door and unlocked it. "After you," he said breathing heavily.

"Spoilsport!" a male voice yelled from across the street.

Micah turned and glared at Dimitri. "Go away!"

"Go where? We live here too," Dimitri responded.

"Yeah, we never get to see Micah actually kiss

a woman. After all the decades of watching him flirt I feel like we should see more," Viktor said grinning.

"Not with my mate you're not," Micah groused.

Serenity was next to him laughing her head off. He turned to her. "You're no help."

Serenity wiggled her fingers at the warriors. "Hi fellas!"

"Hello!" They called back.

Micah racked his brain trying to think of a way to get the warriors to leave them be so they could go inside and hopefully resume what they were doing.

"Micah!" Dimitri yelled pointing.

Seconds later two voices shouted. "*Immobiles!*"

Micah was looking around for the source of danger when Serenity screeched and practically climbed up his back. Her arm around his neck was threatening to cut off his air supply. "Breathe... Serenity... I need to breathe." She loosened her hold but stayed where she was. She pointed down at their feet. "Snake!" she yelled nearly rupturing his ear drum.

Micah looked down and saw a small, bright green snake. "It's just a garden snake," he said leaning down to pick up the frozen reptile.

"Micah hold up," Dimitri said running up with Viktor. Hawthorne and Emlyn right behind them.

"It looks like a harmless garter to me," Micah said.

Viktor raised an eyebrow. "In Noctem Falls?" He pointed to all the stone.

"Good point," Micah said.

Dimitri gave a low whistle. "This is no garter

snake, it is an Eastern Green Mamba and they are deadly."

Behind him his mate kept murmuring the word 'snake' over and over again. He turned to Dimitri. "How'd the hell did it get here?"

Dimitri met his eyes then looked at Serenity. "It is probably someone's exotic pet gotten loose. I will ask around to see where this little guy goes."

Translation. *I will find out what happened and maim whoever is responsible.*

Micah mouthed the words, 'thank you' before turning his head toward his mate. "See my one and only, Dimitri is going to take that little guy home."

Carefully she eased down but stayed behind him her face buried between his shoulder blades. If he wasn't still trying to regulate his own heartbeat he would have found her reaction adorable.

Hawthorne looked over at Serenity. "I'd recommend some of the elderberry wine you smuggled out of your gran's house for your mate Micah."

Serenity peeked around his shoulder, still avoiding looking at Dimitri who held the frozen snake. "Elderberry wine?" she asked looking calmer already.

"Great idea Hawthorne! Come on honey, let's head inside." Micah looked at his warrior brothers. "You have my thanks."

Viktor clapped him on the shoulder. "All in a day's work."

They waved until the guys were out of sight then they headed toward the door. When they got within a foot of the doorway Serenity froze. He easily scooped her up into his arms, unlocked the door again and pushed it open. He eyed the basket and decided to leave it by the door.

"How about we relax in the garden?" he suggested gently setting her on her feet pointing to the back of the house. He closed the door behind them.

She glanced down around their feet still looking spooked. "No snakes, right?"

He tipped her head back and rubbed noses with her. "No snakes I promise."

"Good," she said shuddering. "I swear I can still feel that one against my leg." She convulsed again and started walking to the garden.

Micah clutched at his chest as she opened the large oak door leading to his oasis. The snake had been *on* her? "Elderberry wine, right. Sounds really good right about now." He veered off to the left to the kitchen. He opened the pantry door and rummaged around the bottom shelf until he found his prize. He held up the bottle and blew off the dust. Grinning he stood and went to his cabinets to grab a corkscrew and two glasses.

He found his mate sitting on the large platform bed he had suspended from the ceiling of his large porch. Her knees were tucked under her chin and her feet off the floor. "May I present to you, the best wine in all the world," he said in a grandiose manner, determined to take her mind off that damn snake.

"World?" she asked skeptically.

"Absolutely. I stole... I mean borrowed this from my gran's cellar. She makes the best wine ever." He easily opened the bottle and waved it under her nose allowing the scent to start befuddling her senses.

"It's been magicked!" she exclaimed sitting up letting her feet touch the ground. She reached for one of the empty glasses. "Okay, make a believer out of me," she challenged.

"Don't say I didn't warn you," he said pouring her glass. As she took her first sip he poured his own glass and got comfortable next to her. Using his foot, he kicked off the table and the entire platform began to sway.

She laughed then lifted her feet to scoot even closer to him. "That's why it's suspended."

"Why did you think?" he asked taking a sip.

"That you were a kinky fuck," she said taking another drink.

He choked slightly at her reply. "Serenity!" he said blushing.

"You're blushing!" she crowed.

"You cussed!" he rebutted.

"I do cuss you know."

"You haven't all afternoon."

"I've also been in meetings and healing people too. I don't go around dropping f-bombs willy nilly. I'm used to working in a temple."

"Oh yeah." He took another sip and allowed the warmth to expand down into his stomach. He twirled his finger and a breeze began to circulate around them, bringing the wonderful smells of his garden with it. Jasmine, gardenias and passionflowers were always in bloom here. Feeling lazy he knocked on the wooden arm rest activating the platform and lifted his feet. Their cozy bed continued to sway.

"I love this freaking wine," she said leaning back, her eyes closed.

"It's worth the tongue lashing I get when my gran discovers I've taken a few bottles."

Serenity snorted. "A few?"

"Okay, I cleaned her out during my last visit. Next time I head home she's gonna kill me," he chuckled. "I tell her if she's mad at me, she won't miss me as much."

Serenity propped her head up on her hand turning to face him. "Tell me about your gran."

Micah got comfortable against the pillows. "My gran is my everything. My sperm donor of a father disappeared before I was born, and my mother died in childbirth." He frowned. "There was so much they didn't know about medicine back then. My gran said she probably would have died anyway, even with what we know today. She said she just bled out too fast."

Serenity moved so that she rested her head on his chest. "I'm so sorry to hear about your mom."

"Thank you. I miss what I could have had, but I never really knew her to miss her. Does that make sense?" She nodded. He took a deep breath. "My gran though, she raised me and made sure I knew I was loved every day."

"How?"

"Well, she didn't kill me for one," Micah said then laughed at her expression when she looked up at him. "When I think back on the pranks and shenanigans I used to pull..." He shook his head. "I thank the gods every night for my gran. She also taught me how to use my magic. She never really trusted the Academy, so I didn't go to school like the other kids my age. I stayed at home with my gran learning in her garden."

"But you're not an earth witch," Serenity said.

"Nope, but she is, so was my mother. I'm assuming I got the air magic from my sperm donor. But that doesn't mean I didn't inhale everything she taught me. Though, more than once she had to go next door to get Mr. Compton, an air witch, to pull me out of some scrape I found myself in."

"Like what?"

Micah thought for a moment. "Like the time I accidentally locked myself in mid-air after jumping off of her shed. I think I was five or six at the time. I jumped, panicked and froze. My gran came around the corner and I was six feet off the ground with my mouth wide open from where I screamed. I think I almost killed her that time," he said thoughtfully.

Serenity had to hand him her glass as she laughed. Micah stared down at his mate. "You're going to give me a complex if you keep laughing at me."

"S-s-s-t-top!" she begged crossing her legs.

He sniffed loudly. "Anyway. Mr. Compton heard my gran yelling and rushed over. Needless to say, he laughed himself silly, just like you," he said poking her with one finger careful of her glass.

She sat back up and reached for her glass wiping her eyes. "I can't help it, you must have been absolutely adorable as a child."

Micah nodded. "I was."

"And so modest too," she teased.

He turned to her. "Your turn. What were you like growing up?"

She sipped her wine. "A stubborn, headstrong, willful, adventurous, tomboy. A dark-haired child surrounded by the beautiful golden fae."

"So, you were a handful too?"

She nodded. "My father encouraged me. He was delighted at my magical abilities. But I always felt like I didn't belong." She smiled softly. "I can't tell you how many fights my brother got into defending me. Though between you and me, I started most of the fights."

"Tell me about him, so I can thank him later," Micah said.

"Zachari is my older brother by three minutes. We were the first set of twins born in Eiré Danu in over a millennium. The queen herself sent my parents birthing gifts. He's tall and beautiful like my Papa. He's also kind and loyal. No matter what trouble I caused he always took up for me even when I was in the wrong."

"What'd you do?"

"Accidentally cut some of the queen's favorite flowers to give to my mother, not knowing that they were protected."

"Yikes."

"Luckily the queen was very forgiving. If I had to be honest, I think she indulged me more than my parents. I think I entertained her."

"I overheard a conversation between her and Etain once, she sounded like a wonderful person."

She nodded. "Oh, she really is. There were so many times where she made it a point to hold my hand during a function or have me sit beside her during tea, just to show others she didn't think I was any less fae because of my hair," she ran a hand over her brown locks.

She looked lost in thought for a moment then giggled. "Her consort Brennus used to sneak me candy when my parents weren't looking." She smiled up at him. "I always shared with Zach though." Her expression became thoughtful before poked him gently. "What were you supposed to go over with me?"

Micah swirled his wine in his glass. "Adriel offered all of the Eta Unit homes within the Ambrosios quarters on Level One. If we decide to stay in Noctem Falls, we have a choice of either staying here or moving in with the rest of my unit on the royal level."

She stared down into her glass. "I think it's a pretty safe assumption that my position as the Water Temple head has already been terminated." She looked around. "I think living on Level One comes with too many perks to turn down, but I would hate to give up your garden."

Micah felt sorry that his mate had probably already lost her position but was ecstatic that she already liked his garden. "Adriel completely gutted the Ambrosios quarters. Instead of walking into an antechamber you find yourself on a small road. Along each wall he left space for two smaller homes, then at the end of the road they put two large buildings side by side. One estate is for Gavriel, the other is for Adriel. The four spaces on either side of the cobblestone path are for the Eta Unit."

"Is it because you're the ranking unit?" she asked.

Micah shook his head. "No, it's because Adriel is the biggest closet softie I have ever met, and he would have missed us."

"He seems so proper."

"Trust me, whatever that man feels, he feels

deeply. Plus with most of our mates tied to Level One, it just made sense to live down there too," he explained.

"What do you mean?

"Well, Eva is pretty much the liaison for the refugees. Not only does the Wolftown pack trust her, all the other refugees look to her to act as their voice. She's kick ass enough to hold her own and they know it. Then there's Kari. I'm just going to be honest, she pretty much runs the city. That's how much Magnus relies on her. She's like a little general behind the scenes telling us all what to do. After Kari, we got Ellie, then Vivi. They will probably get their own labs next to Broderick's. Magnus is no fool, I bet before he got sick he was writing up a list of stuff needed for them to be happy and stay right here and that was before he knew Vivi was his goddsdaughter. Then there's you." He smiled at her. "With the miniature baby boom in Noctem Falls, I bet he will try to bribe you to stay as well. He goes absolutely nuts for the kids." He took another sip of his wine. "So, you see, being on Level One just makes sense."

Serenity looked at him blinking slowly. He could tell she was getting sleepy. "Can we keep your garden? And your swing? And your wine?"

He gently kissed her nose. "Of course."

"You have a nose fetish," she said giggling. "Or you missed my mouth."

"Well, we can't have that," he said before kissing her slowly. When he leaned back she sighed happily. She picked up her glass and drained it before letting it tip over beside her. Smiling she closed her eyes again. "I love your garden."

Micah picked up her glass, then finished his own wine before leaning over to place both empty glasses beside the bottle on the end table.

"Drunk?" he asked, snuggling in beside her.

"No. Just..." she trailed off.

"Completely relaxed, carefree and perfectly content?"

She nodded rubbing her nose playfully on his chest. "I think it did something to the mating pull," she said, before she yawned.

Micah nodded giving in to the lull of peacefulness threatening to overtake him. "I think it sped it up."

She nodded again. "Yup."

"Yup," he echoed.

"Love you Micah."

"Love you too, my one and only," he replied as his eyes finally drifted close.

Serenity woke up and looked around. They were still in Micah's magical, Disney-like garden. Her prince was currently snoring softly as their bed swayed back and forth.

She stared down at him, then remembered their confessions before falling asleep. She expected panic to overtake her at any moment, but nothing happened. If anything, watching his sleeping face snore and drool slightly had her smiling and feeling content. She eyed the bottle of wine. That stuff was potent and needed a warning label. She grinned.

They were so drinking some of that later, maybe after dinner.

"Dinner!" she exclaimed.

She shook her mate. "Micah! Micah wake up! What time is it?"

Micah opened his eyes then blinked. "Why did you wake me up to ask me what time it was?"

Serenity hopped off the bed and pulled out her phone. "It's five thirty! We have less than a half an hour to get ready for dinner."

Micah was looking much more alert now. "Shit, I forgot all about dinner." He stretched. "If there wasn't so much going on I'd try to tempt you to stay here."

Serenity shook her head. "No way. I need to, at the very least, check in with Vivi regarding the progress she made testing Aiden's blood." She looked around frantically. "Where's my bag?"

Micah threaded his hands behind his head. "Where we left it, on Level One."

Serenity looked down at her utilitarian white button-down shirt and jeans. "I can't wear this to dinner!"

"Why not? Meryn showed up to dinner last night in Pikachu pajamas."

"That's Meryn, you gave me a list a mile long why she can get away with it," she countered. She gasped. "You never told me what everyone's rank was."

Micah shrugged. "I don't think it matters, they're mostly family now anyway."

She looked down at her mate. "What will you wear?"

Micah gave her a shit-eating grin. "I'm changing

into my uniform."

"Ugh! I hate you!"

"No you don't. You love me, you said so your-self," he said smugly.

She paused in her meltdown. "Not too weird?"

He shook his head. "Nope. Neither one of us is fighting this mating, plus the wine knocked down any barriers we may have had up." He nodded. "I think we skipped right to being able to fart in front of each other."

Serenity felt her mouth drop. "I will never, ever fart in front of you."

Micah chuckled. "Yes, you will, and it will be cute."

"I can't do you right now!" she exclaimed, throwing her hands up. "Maybe I can sneak down and grab my bag and change down there?"

"*Or* you can head to the bathroom to freshen up, I'll call the twins on the walkie-talkie and have them run get your bag, and bring it to you," Micah suggested.

"Why didn't you say that to begin with?" she demanded.

"Because you're sexy when you're sassy," he replied almost immediately.

"Right. Call them." She looked around. "Where's the bathroom?"

"Upstairs, the master is the only room on the left," he replied.

She was about to take her first step toward the house when she turned and hopped onto the bed to lay across him. "Fate knew what she was doing when she gave you to me," she said before leaning down to kiss him.

Before he could wrap his arms around her, she popped up and opened the door. "Hurry up and call the twins," she ordered leaving her mate looking decidedly rattled. She was glad her kiss worked, there was no way she was going to leave him looking so damn smug. Grinning she jogged up the stairs to his bathroom.

CHAPTER SIX

SERENITY FELT A THOUSAND TIMES better about her simple black dress when she saw Meryn in the antechamber in a pair of sweats and a hoodie. Micah leaned down following her line of sight. "I told you."

She jabbed him in the stomach and smiled when he grunted. "What was that?" she asked.

"You look beautiful," he wheezed.

"Thank you. You look very handsome in your uniform," she said smiling up at him brightly.

Before Micah could say anything, Declan reached between them holding up his hand. Grinning she gave him a high five.

"Hey!" Micah protested.

"She has your number brother and I have to say it's fun to watch you flounder," Declan admitted.

Mentally Serenity went over everyone's names in her head. She didn't know how Pip managed to learn them so quickly. As she surveyed the room she saw him standing beside Meryn, looking around like he was lost.

She made her way over to them and placed a

hand on his shoulder. Using her magic she calmed him down a bit. He smiled up at her. "Thank you. Meryn said that I do not have to be afraid of anyone, but..." his eyes trailed around the room. She could see what he meant.

Everyone here looked official, important, royal. The unit warriors in their everyday clothes were impressive, in their uniforms they seemed even larger and more intimidating. The women, with the exception of Meryn, wore simple cocktail dresses and looked polished. She leaned down. "Can you help me keep their names straight?" she asked.

Pip's chest puffed out at her request. "Yes. I can do that."

Now that he had a task he seemed to come out of his shell. He gently took her hand and walked her around the room re-introducing her to everyone.

The men smiled down at Pip and clapped him on the back telling him he was doing a wonderful job. Micah nodded his approval and thanked him for looking out for her. Every compliment seemed to peel back a tiny layer to Pip's personality. Finally he frowned and pointed. "That is Sebastian, but I do not know who is with him. No one told me his name yet."

Serenity looked across the antechamber to see that Prince Magnus had just stepped into the room pulling down on his sleeves while frowning. Sebastian hovered behind him like an overprotective hen.

"Sebastian, please leave it be. It will be fine for tonight," Prince Magnus pleaded as Sebastian fretted over the prince's ill-fitting clothing.

Sebastian sighed dramatically. "I never even noticed you grew!"

"Uncle!" Beth exclaimed and launched herself at the prince.

A warm smile transformed his face as he easily caught his niece and comforted her. "Shush now Bethy, I am well." He took a step back and flexed his arm grinning. "Stronger than ever." When he flexed his other arm they all heard fabric tear and Sebastian looked faint. "I-I-I..."

Magnus just shrugged off his dinner jacket and rolled up the sleeves of his button down shirt. "Much better." He winked at Meryn. "Maybe I should try sweat pants later," he said in a teasing voice. Serenity thought it was adorable the way he said sweatpants as two different words.

Beth kept wiping at her eyes. "Are you sure you should be up?"

The prince nodded. "Sebastian has been pouring blood down my throat all afternoon. I am ready for some real food."

Serenity watched as Meryn inched over to Sebastian and pulled on his sleeve. She pointed to Vivi and the squire gasped. "Of course."

Sebastian walked over to his charge. "Magnus, there is someone here I would like you to meet." He motioned for Vivi to step forward.

Prince Magnus frowned. "I already met Vivi, Sebastian. I was not sick that long."

Sebastian gave him a flat look before continuing. "As I was saying. Magnus I would like you to meet Vivian Mercy, Mercia DuCoeur's daughter and your goddaughter," Sebastian crowed.

The prince's mouth dropped open. Shyly Vivi

held up a small cloth pony. "You have no idea how wonderful it is to see you again...Maggie," she whispered.

The prince of the vampires wept openly as he pulled her into his arms. "I thought we had lost you! I had warriors searching for you for years," he said choking on the words. Beth and Meryn kept passing a tissue between the two of them as they watched Vivi and the prince.

"Hal kept me safe," Vivi said using her cloth pony to wipe away her tears.

Prince Magnus stared at the little stuffy. "You still have her?"

Hal sniffled and wiped his nose on a towel. "It's one of her most prized possessions."

Meryn shook her head and popped over to Magnus. "Let's keep the introductions coming." She pointed to Warrick. "Warrick Fortier the newest Founding Family head of Noctem Falls. We totally arrested DeLaFontaine and dissolved his house."

Prince Magnus' eyes bugged out slightly. "You what?"

Meryn continued. "We arrested Jervasius too, for being an absolute jerk." She motioned for Pip to step forward. He inched closer looking a bit scared. Meryn dragged him next to her. "This is Pip Maverick, DeLaFontaine was his sperm donor, but I've adopted him."

The prince looked around the room a bit wild-eyed. "What? How long was I sick again?" he demanded.

Beth winced. "That was a very 'tear the band-aid off' type of update for someone who has been ill."

Adriel stepped forward. "Gavriel, Vivian and

I have publicly claimed our heritage and have reopened the Ambrosios and DuCoeur residences here on Level One. I made room for the Eta Unit to move into the Ambrosios quarters given how much our mates are involved in the operations down here."

Eva grinned and stepped beside her mate. "Pavil Desrosiers is the Ambrosios squire. We stole him from the Régis family after we found out that Jervasius forced Bree to be his mate despite being actually mated to Pavil. Pavil runs the house, but Bree runs our schedule."

Warrick and Avery moved closer. "I am trying to get my uncle removed as head of the DuBois family. There is too much bad blood between him and the people of Level Five to keep him in a position of leadership."

Pip nodded. "He is mean and helps the other mean men take people away when they are bad," he added.

Ellie leaned closer to Prince Magnus. "DeLa-Fontaine also ordered the jerk tunnel escort to kill Vivi," she contributed.

Vivi scowled. "He almost killed my baby," she looked up at Etain who wrapped himself around her. "But Etain and the other fae helped save her." She smiled at her *athair*. "I'm pregnant by the way."

Serenity walked over and placed a hand on the prince's shoulder. She lowered his heart rate and calmed him down. "There, there Prince Magnus, it's all good news," she said soothingly.

He turned to face her and smiled. "I remember your magic. You chased away the darkness, so I could wake up." He covered her hand with his own. "Thank you for the help. I do not think I could have freed myself without your assistance." He looked around the room until his eyes landed on Micah. "She is yours I assume?"

Micah walked over to stand next to his mate. "Actually, I am hers," he said, before kissing her temple.

Prince Magnus chuckled. "I always knew you were smart Micah." He turned to her. "Please call me Magnus, especially considering we will be neighbors."

She smiled. "I'd like to introduce my two best friends." She looked to the edges of the room and motioned for them to come forward. Laelia dropped a small curtsy and Radclyffe bowed.

"These are Laelia and Radclyffe, two of the best healers in Storm Keep," she said, smiling encouragingly at her friends.

Magnus greeted them warmly then turned to her with a questioning look. "How did you get here?"

Sebastian cleared his throat. "Might I suggest moving to the dining room before launching into many more explanations," he eyed Magnus. "Your food will get cold."

Magnus rubbed his hands together. "I feel like I could eat everything you set before me." He snaked an arm around Beth and one around Vivi before kissing each of them on the cheek. "I am still very feeble and need assistance getting to the dining room," he said pouting at both women.

They laughed and leaned their heads on his shoulders. Beth patted him on the chest. "Of course, uncle, we'll help you."

Etain and Gavriel followed, looking decidedly grumpy without their mates. Serenity hung back as everyone made their way to the table. Marjoram stopped in front of her on her way to join the others. "They never really grow up," she looked at Micah. "Some less than others."

"Oh Marjoram, my ripest little berry. I know you will be desolate without me," Micah teased.

Serenity was shocked to see the older woman blush. In earlier interactions she had been put together and in charge.

Marjoram swatted at Micah. "You better take care of this young lady Micah Sageson, don't make me call your grandmother," she threatened.

Micah paled. "You know my gran?"

Marjoram gave him a sly smile. "I looked her up after meeting you. She told me to tell you that you are in big trouble for taking her wine."

Micah gulped. "It was only a few bottles," he mumbled.

Marjoram raised an elegant brow. "A few bottles? She said you emptied her entire cellar."

Serenity turned to him. "You have an entire cellar's worth?" she asked eagerly.

"Maybe," he said eyeing Marjoram.

The older woman held up two fingers. "Two bottles and I'll smooth things over with your gran by offering her my snickerdoodle recipe and gush over you meeting your mate."

Micah looked relieved. "Deal!" he agreed immediately.

She met Serenity's eyes and winked before disappearing behind the closed dining room door. Micah turned to her grinning. "She is amazing.

Maybe my gran won't kill me now."

"What's this about wine?" Laelia asked.

Serenity gave Micah puppy dog eyes. He sighed. "Of course, they can have a bottle."

Serenity looped her arm through Laelia's and headed toward the dining room. "Let me tell you about the best wine in the entire world."

Once everyone was seated Micah was amazed to see they had actually filled the long, royal dining table. He watched as Hal, Ryuu, Pavil and Sebastian served everyone effortlessly. Of course, with this many seated for dinner you would almost need four squires. He'd attended balls with fewer people.

He sat back as everyone seemed to talk at once. Slowly Magnus was brought up to speed. Kari, bless her, once seated had presented Magnus with his iPad and went over the itemized list of changes.

Serenity leaned in. "They're so happy."

He pulled her close remembering the awful evening Magnus fell ill. "We needed this. Everyone has had so much thrown at them, we truly needed this joy. Having Magnus back with us changes everything." He kissed her nose. "You're my miracle."

"May I have everyone's attention please?" Rex asked standing. He raised his glass. "I would like to propose a toast to..." He paused dramatically. "To Fate. Not only has she provided our warriors with mates who will be the salvation of us all, she has also introduced us to new friends who have become family and has blessed us with the start of the next generation. Though our fight isn't over to drive back the sickness amongst us, I have no doubt that this family will overcome."

Declan stood his eyes bright. "To family!" He raised his glass. Around the table everyone stood and raised their glass high.

"To family!" everyone cheered before draining their glasses.

After everyone sat down Pip turned to Meryn. "Me too?" he asked.

Meryn nodded. "Absolutely."

"Pip," Magnus said softly getting the young man's attention.

Pip turned to the prince his eyes wide. "I am sorry my father made you sick. That was bad of him. And I am sorry he called you a weak fool, that was mean."

Magnus looked a bit surprised at Pip's apology then chuckled. "You have nothing to be sorry for." He glanced down at his iPad. "After hearing your story, I feel like I have to apologize to you Pip. I never really looked into why you acted the way you did. You and others like you suffered because politics got in the way of me doing the right thing." He looked from Adriel to Gavriel then back to Pip. "Luckily I have very good friends who are helping to straighten things out. Can you forgive me for not seeing how you were being treated?"

By the end of the apology Pip was trembling so badly he looked like he was about to fly apart. Meryn looked around the table. "What do I do?" she asked.

"Hug him Meryn. It will make him feel better,"

Serenity advised.

Meryn scrunched her nose at the word hug, but she nevertheless wrapped an arm around her distraught friend.

Magnus looked hurt. "I did not mean to upset him."

Pip buried his face in Meryn's shoulder and shook his head back and forth. "No. This is wrong, I am nothing, I am bad. The prince should not say such things to me," he whispered.

Magnus' face became unreadable. He turned to Warrick. "You have my permission to restructure Level Five however you see fit. If you need to establish new Noble houses let me know. I never, ever want another citizen of mine to believe they are nothing," Magnus bit off the final word.

Warrick nodded. "It will be done."

Pip looked up his face drenched with tears. "New Noble families?" he asked.

Warrick nodded. "I am trying to get rid of all the bad men." The giant man said softly trying not to upset Pip anymore. "But the people are afraid of me, so I am having a hard time figuring out who the bad men are."

Pip sat up straighter. "I can help. I know all the bad men, even the scary ones who used to live in the Pits."

Around the table everyone quieted. Meryn turned to Pip. "Say what?"

Pip looked around. "That is where the scary bad men used to live, who ate people."

Aiden leaned in. "What else Pip? We don't know anything about those men, so whatever you tell us could help everyone." Like Warrick, Aiden made sure to keep his tone even.

Pip ducked his head. "Sometimes I was bad and listened when father had his meetings, it was the best way to know how to make him happy so I could have food."

At the end of the table they heard wood crack as Magnus snapped off the arm to his chair. He gave Pip a smile. "Do not mind me. This chair is old. Please continue." He let the wood fall to the floor.

Pip nodded. "After the wolfies got here father was furious when the bad men ate some people on Level Six. He said they were going to ruin everything. I heard him tell the nasty tunnel escort to kidnap someone from Level Six so that the wolfies would think *he* killed the refugees. After that he started sending bad people from our level to the Pits for the scary bad men to eat." He looked at Meryn. "That is why you have to be careful not to say bad things on Level Five or you get sent down to the Pits."

"My gods!" Adriel choked out the words. He turned to his mate. "It was not Augustus Pettier who attacked you in the Pits, it was one of those monsters."

Gavriel's eyes burned scarlet. "How many scary bad men were there Pip?"

Pip shrugged. "I do not know. But there were enough that when they left the city the tunnel escort had to use a platform to get them to the Grand Hall."

Aiden sat back. "The door alarm, when Marek was knocked unconscious during the attack on Vivi."

Colton nodded then looked over at Vivi. "Looks

like killing you was meant to be a distraction."

"How in the hell did they get in?" Magnus exploded. "Why do any of this?" Like Gavriel his eyes were burning red.

"The blood. They took the older blood," Vivi whispered.

Magnus paled. "How much?"

Vivi began to shake. "Dozens of bags."

"Oh my god," Meryn whispered.

"I know love," Aiden said sympathetically, pulling her close. Meryn leaned away from her mate. "No. Not that." She looked around the table. "We were motherfucking played!"

Pip looked at Meryn. "Yeah! Motherfucking played!" he shouted before leaning down. "How?"

Meryn stared at Pip. "I freaking love you right now."

Pip beamed. "Because I am your brother."

"And you're awesome." She turned to Magnus. "I think the random attacks in the area were to get you to open the city. I think those bastards piggy-backed into the city when the first batch of refugees arrived. We ended up using platforms to lower the wolves into the city because there were so many of them, if our killers were invisible, then we wouldn't have seen them," she paused. "We really need to figure out a way to modify my flour glue spell so it doesn't ruin shit."

Serenity exchanged looks with Laelia and Radclyffe before speaking up. "Vampire blood has to be one of the most potent substances in the paranormal world. Unfortunately, there are probably dozens of ways to use it illegally and they're all bad."

"Oh!" Kendrick gasped. "Oh! Oh!"

Anne blinked. "I'm not sure I want to know whatever he's figured out. He's never at a loss for words."

Kendrick simply rested his forehead on the table. Serenity looked from Laelia, to Anne to Meryn then to Law. Whatever Kendrick was about to say would be horrible.

Kendrick sat up and turned to Ryuu.

Ryuu waved at him. "On it," he said heading to the kitchen. Without asking Hal, Sebastian and Pavil were hot on his heels.

Magnus rubbed a hand over his mouth. "Can I assume they are retrieving something that will make whatever you are about tell us easier to face?"

Kendrick nodded looking ill. Beth stared. "Is this worse than discovering the beads were made from the souls of the murdered unborn babies?"

"What!" Serenity demanded.

Beth covered her mouth with her hands. "I am so sorry, you didn't know."

"What?" Laelia and Radclyffe echoed.

Kendrick turned to Kari. "While Ryuu fetches us something that will keep us sane, can you get everyone at this table on the same page?"

Kari stood and began going over the events start-ing with the feral attacks in Lycaonia. As she kept talking Serenity felt her world shatter into thou-sands of pieces. Beside her Micah rubbed her back soothingly as Kari revealed the most tragic events she had ever heard.

Kari wiped at her eyes as she finished, causing Declan to stand and pull her close. "Wonderful job baby," he murmured, easing her back into her chair.

"Here we go," Ryuu announced coming in from the kitchen. He pushed a cart that held a tray of what looked to be shot glasses and steaming cups of tea. Behind him the other squires held identical trays in their hands as they made their way around the room.

Hal placed a generously filled shot glass with amber liquid next to the tea cup in front of her. She looked around the table, everyone, with the exception of the pregnant women, had both alcohol and tea. She leaned over the cup and smiled. She turned to Kendrick. "Blessed Chamomile, from your own stash no less."

Kendrick stared down at his shot glass. "I hate to say it, but this has been needed too much as of late."

Magnus raised his shot glass. "Let us do this."

Around the table sputters, gasps and cursing was heard as everyone downed their shots.

Serenity thought that whatever she just drank was burning her esophagus down to her stomach. She was about to complain when everything tilted for a second then blurred pleasantly. "Oh my." Sighs filled the air as the potent alcohol took effect.

Kendrick waited until they were sipping the tea before he cast a soundproofing spell. Serenity knew that whatever he was about to say was important because he poured a hefty amount of power into the spell. She opened her mouth wide trying to get her ears to pop.

Kendrick stood. "As Kari explained, during one of last feral attacks on the city, Lycaonia lost their witch Elder, Rowan Airgead. Right before he died he managed to pass on what he thought the enemy was after." He closed his eyes. "He said that mated paranormals were needed for an army. Witches for fuel," he looked at Magnus. "And Vampires for blood."

"What for?" Magnus asked.

Kendrick swallowed hard. "I have no evidence, but, I think that vampire blood is used to create those damn necklaces. They already harvested dozens of shifter souls from around Lycaonia and damn near drained my godsdaughter of her magic. My best friends who are Law and Amelia's brothers are on their hit list to get more magic. I think they are combining vampire blood, witch's magic, an unborn's soul as a vessel and a shifter's soul for their abilities to create as many necklaces as they need to infiltrate our society and break it down from the inside out." He sat back down looking uncharacteristically defeated.

"Fuck that. Ryuu, I think I need that shot," Meryn said, looking at her squire. He shook his head. "It is too potent for the baby, but I did arrange for dessert." He dropped a kiss on her forehead and reached under the cart to pull out bowls of what looked to be a small mountain of chocolate.

Meryn sighed. "You do love me." She picked up her spoon and dug in. The squires passed out the desserts and everyone reached for the treats, dinner long forgotten. It was quiet as everyone slowly ate their chocolatey comfort and absorbed what Kendrick divulged.

"And I practically handed them the blood they needed. I played right into their hands," Magnus whispered.

"They're smart, I'll give them that," Meryn said,

licking her spoon.

All eyes swung to her. "What do you mean?" Kari asked.

Meryn twirled her spoon around as she spoke. "Well if they tried to use brute force to gather vampire blood, like the guerrilla attacks in Lycaonia, it would have taken them months, maybe even years to get a decent amount. Ninety-percent of the vampire population is stacked up in Noctem Fall's beehive. But by infiltrating the city and introducing a virus where the only possible cure is older vampire blood all they had to do was sit back and wait for us to try and cure the city. Then they could pack up the blood we gathered in neat little bags and leave." She shook her head. "We know they've been gathering shifter souls for over twenty years, to gather so much vampire blood I bet their necklace production timeline got skewed when Lycaonia got sealed."

Laelia nodded. "It's like when you're baking. You start with the component that takes the longest to prepare. Like making sure the cream cheese is room temperature. That can take hours, so you do that first. Then after that you can simply add the other ingredients and blend. Considering the first component is an unborn's soul, they would have to wait for shifters to turn up pregnant. Which as everyone knows is hit or miss at best. Most paranormals have a hard time even finding their mates."

Magnus turned to Aiden. "The spell, the one for the warriors to find their mates."

Aiden nodded looking sick. "We believe that the matriarchs were influenced to request that spell."

Meryn took a sip of her tea. "I'd love to meet

the one orchestrating this. Every time we learn something, the web becomes a little bigger. We're dealing with a freaking genius."

Aiden looked down at her. "Can you please not be impressed by the psychopath trying to destroy all we know?"

Meryn waved her spoon in Aiden's face. "Hey, genius is genius. Think about it. That spell was specifically designed to target the unit warriors. The warriors meet their mates, get them knocked up. The bad guys kill the mates. If the men or mates were shifters they get the unborn's soul as a vessel, possibly an ability from the mother and a blood-thirsty, insane, unit trained warrior to unleash on us later. If the men or mates are vampires or witches they harvest the blood and the magic. The more unit warrior mates you kill, the fewer warriors there are available to defend the pillar cities later. It's like a win-win-win-win scenario for them." She paused. "Mostly." She took another huge bite of her chocolate mountain and hummed happily completely oblivious of the horrified stares she was receiving from around the table.

Pip looked around at everyone's expressions and frowned. He hopped out of his seat and stood in front of her. "She is not bad"

Aiden blinked. "Oh, Pip. We don't think she's bad. We're upset she said something that should have been evident to us all along. It's something terrible so we're a bit shaken, but we're grateful for her pointing it out."

Pip's lower lip trembled. "You were staring."

Meryn pulled Pip back into his chair. "Say ahhhh!"

Pip opened his mouth dutifully. "Ahhh."

Meryn shoved her chocolate filled spoon in his mouth. "Thank you for defending me."

Pip's eyes widened as he chewed. Serenity was seriously concerned for the small vampire when his eyes rolled back in his head. Meryn chuckled. "I know right."

Pip quickly swallowed. "I did not try any because it looked like poop. What is it? It makes me feel like heaven!" He picked up his spoon and dug in.

"It's chocolate Pip. Besides coffee, it's one of the best substances on earth," Laelia explained.

Aiden nodded. "Chocolate is very powerful."

Everyone watched Pip and Meryn eat their dessert and somehow despite the horrendous things they discovered, everyone was smiling.

"I don't know if it's the Blessed Chamomile, but I feel like I should be sadder than I am," Serenity said pointing at Meryn.

Micah smiled. "Lately I have found that it's easier to face the darkest of moments when you share the burden with loved ones." He indicated to everyone seated around the table. "What we learned tonight truly terrifies me for the future, but I know I am not alone. Each one of us lightens the load and in small ways chips away at our enemy's plans. I bet DeLaFontaine never imagined his deepest secrets would be revealed by the amazing son he ignored. His life choice to mistreat Pip led us to tonight." He made sure Pip met his eyes. "Every single person born has a role to play and is precious to Fate. Never forget that Pip. Your help could be the turning point to save our entire world."

Pip looked stunned. "Me?"

Warrick nodded. "Yes you, and Meryn too. She was smart enough to see how special you are. What if the two of you never crossed paths?"

Pip shook his head. "I do not want to think about that. It would make me sad."

Meryn smiled slyly at Micah. "That's what I meant when I said that it was 'mostly' a win-win scenario. I bet they never factored in the warriors' mates being so kick ass." She pointed to her chest. "I beat sense into Aiden,"

"Hey!" Aiden protested.

Meryn continued. "Beth got us organized, Rheia saved Colton and helped figure out the necklaces, Amelia survived being drained and was able to tell us what the enemy had planned, Anne was everyone's rock when we discovered the beads being unborn babies." She looked over at Eva. "Here in Noctem Falls Eva abandoned me to become the voice for the refugees." Eva snorted, and Meryn kept going. "Kari, I don't even think I can wrap up all the good she's done keep us on track, Ellie, Vivi and Serenity have worked miracles keeping everyone alive. The virus probably should have plunged the city into chaos, but the city has become stronger and better than before." Meryn took a deep breath looking a bit embarrassed. "All I'm saying is maybe the enemy's supposed power play in getting the warriors mated is actually our power play." Around the table the women were sitting straighter as if filled with a grander purpose and the men radiated a hope that hadn't been there just moments before.

Magnus turned to Sebastian. "That child gets whatever she wants, whenever she wants it." Sebastian nodded as he beamed down at Meryn looking like a proud parent.

Meryn winked at Magnus. "You do that anyway."

Aiden shot a desperate look to Magnus. "Can we put some parameters on that?"

"No way! Magnus can spoil me whenever!" Meryn fussed.

"Maybe our biggest weapon is the smallest of us," Kendrick whispered as Meryn argued with her mate. Nearly everyone around the table heard him except for the small human who could quite possibly be the salvation of them all.

CHAPTER SEVEN

SERENITY STARED UP AT THE impossible night sky above Micah's garden. "I feel like everything has changed."

He stretched out beside her as the bed rocked them back and forth. "Everything has changed, yet nothing has changed. Everything is exactly as we left it when we went to dinner, but our perceptions are different."

She turned to face him. "Doesn't it scare you that someone or something is out there trying to destroy us?"

He reached out and pulled her into the curve of his body. "Not really, but then again, I'm trained to expect that everything is trying to destroy me."

She just grunted and rested her head on his bicep. "Well, I've always believed that the council was out to get me, does that count?" she asked playfully looking up at him.

He had the type of face where his expression changed how you saw him. Usually he was smiling, laughing, or teasing. His eyes would light up and he looked safe, dependable and kind. But when he dropped his guard, his expression became pensive, dark and intense.

She wanted to kiss along his sexy jawline and see the heat flare in his eyes. In less than a day she had seen so many different sides to her mate, except one. She was desperate to see what his face would look like as he drove his body into hers as they both drowned in lust.

She rolled him onto his back and straddled him her black dress riding up to rest on her thighs.

He smiled up at her. She huffed. He still looked playful. Throwing caution to the wind she pulled her dress up over her head and threw it on the ground. She reached behind her and released the clasp to her bra letting it fall beside them. She cupped her breasts and offered them to him.

His expression darkened and he looked up at her with hooded eyes. "What do you want of me?" he asked, raising up so that he held his upper body off the bed with his core strength alone. With his hands free he was able to trace her collarbones gently.

"Just you Micah. I want my mate without the smile. I want you at your worst so that you know, no matter what, I will always want you."

He snapped his fingers and she felt a warm stream of air around her wrists. Slowly her arms were pulled over her head and she was lifted off the platform until her toes barely scraped the covers. She was suspended but wasn't being pulled down by her own body weight. It was as if the air cradled her in place for his perusal.

"Micah?" she asked, as he rose to his knees loosening his tie.

"Only you can see me like this," he whispered.

Wordlessly he finished undressing and dropped his clothes to the floor. He knelt before her completely nude and she couldn't help but stare, he was absolute beauty personified. He wasn't tall like Etain or broad like Grant and Declan. It was as if every square inch of him was designed with perfection in mind. He had a slight golden undertone to his skin that looked like a permanent tan. His chest, arms and legs were covered in a thin layer of light brown hair and his shoulders were broad without being wide. Her eyes traveled downward and it got even better, his abdomen was cut and each muscle defined with gentle dips and ridges. She looked at his face, it was her favorite part of his body. "You are without a doubt the most stunning creature I have ever seen. Men like you must have inspired Michelangelo and encouraged the existence of demigods."

He gave her a wolfish grin. "That beautiful compliment earned you a treat."

"Treat?" she asked as he slid her panties down her hips and pulled them free.

Gently her legs were pulled apart and he ran his tongue along the seam her folds made. "Micah," she breathed.

He dipped his tongue between her folds and found her clit. He suckled the tiny nub lazily. She felt her body begin to tighten.

"Micah!" she called out urgently, trying to twist her body so she could increase the friction. He was slowly driving her crazy.

His hands came up and he dug his fingers into her ass cheeks to hold her still. She felt her legs begin to shake and when he surprised her by bit-ing down gently on her clit she flew apart.

"One," he said leaning back a satisfied look on his face.

"Oh gods," she croaked.

He winked. "Maybe just us demigods."

She thought now that her 'treat' was over he would lower her to the platform. She was shocked when his body rose to meet hers midair. He wrapped her legs around his waist and buried his face between her neck and shoulder.

"My one and only," he said softly.

"Make love to me Micah," she begged. "I need to feel my mate."

He pulled back and cupped her face with his hands. "I wish we could freeze time and stay in this moment forever."

She flexed her legs and rubbed her dripping core over his stomach. "If we are to freeze time, I'd rather you be inside of me for that lasting moment," she teased.

He chuckled. "Never say I don't give you what you ask for," he warned. He reached between them and guided his hot length between her slick folds. With a snap of his hips he drove himself deep inside of her.

"Yes!" she hissed.

He was relentless as he set the pace. She struggled at her air bonds and her hands were released. She wrapped her arms around his neck and held on.

Defying gravity, Micah made love to her as if desperation fueled his efforts. As the pleasure built between them she suddenly began to see fragments of moments.

Her laughing as he spilled his basket of fries on the floor giving her a pouty face. Him hiding in the shower to scare the hell out of her when she went pee. Lazy mornings eating breakfast in bed. Her throwing paint brushes at him in frustration while decorating their home. The look on his face when the pregnancy stone glowed amber. And making love. Thousands of moments of them making love compiled into one experience.

As he thrust for the last time roaring his release, she simply shattered as pleasure consumed her. Their souls rose up and whirled together, each holding a tiny piece of magic. When they settled into their bodies she could not only feel Micah, but also a bit of his air magic as well.

She tried to even her breathing but couldn't. She was sobbing but it was from pure happiness. What she saw, what they experienced could only be described as spiritual. Under her hands Micah shook as his hot tears trailed down her neck.

Slowly they drifted down to the swinging bed.

"I am never letting you go," he said sounding choked up.

"Well you'll have to eventually, especially if we're going to clean up," she said running her hands through his hair.

He pulled from her body and they both groaned. Every single nerve ending was still vibrating. His arms trembled then collapsed leaving him face down on the mattress beside her.

"Can you breathe?" she asked.

"No," was his muffled reply.

Laughing she rolled him to one side. As she scooted to the edge of the platform she ran her hand where her body was just lying.

"How? It's not even sweaty?"

Micah grinned. "Self-cleaning sheets. Leif perfected them for Vivi. Since he owed me a favor I got the next sets for the platform and the bed upstairs."

Serenity squirmed and made a face at him. "It didn't clean me. I'm heading to the shower."

Micah waved her on. "When I get feeling back in my extremities I'll join you."

She shook her head. "Poor baby."

"Feel free to start again without me. I'll try to make it up there before you finish."

"No offense, because you literally rocked my universe, but I don't think I can handle any more tonight. I feel like we had a lifetime's worth of orgasms when we claimed one another."

Micah frowned and she laughed. "Don't worry Romeo, I'm sure we'll both feel better tomorrow."

She blew him a kiss and headed inside to clean up.

He tried to stay calm as she walked away. There was no way Fate gave them a lifetime in one moment because he was going to lose his mate. His nightmares haunted him as he reclined on the platform staring up at the false night sky.

He didn't care if he had to fight the gods themselves. He wouldn't lose his mate, he'd save her, even from herself.

Serenity stretched out beside her mate, in their bed, for their first night together. The room was dark except for a tiny globe that looked like a miniature moon. The soft glow was comforting and illuminated the room just enough so she wouldn't stub her toe in the middle of the night going to the bathroom. She rolled on to one side and studied her mate's face.

Their claiming had been nothing like she'd ever heard of. It hadn't affected just her body, but her heart and mind as well. Each one of those fragments had become like memories to her. She felt in her soul that she and Micah were mated years instead of hours. Were they premonitions of moments to come? She snorted as she remembered aiming a paintbrush at his head.

"What?" Micah asked turning to face her.

"I was remembering how I threw the paintbrush at you when we were decorating the nursery."

"Was it for the nursery?" he asked. "All I got from that moment was my frantic efforts to calm you down."

She reached up and traced his lips. "Yup, it was for the nursery."

His smile turned goofy then he frowned fiercely. "Childbirth is traumatic, I don't think I could handle watching your pain. Couldn't we just lay an egg?"

She rolled her eyes. "When the time comes Laelia will be with us, Radclyffe too. We'll be fine."

Micah brightened. "Do they know a spell to pop the baby out without all the screaming and blood?"

"No, but they'll keep me from killing you."

"Definitely a good thing," he said.

"Micah?" she said softly, wondering if she should ask about her nightmares.

"Yes? My one and only."

"Did you have dreams before you met me?"

He frowned and simply nodded.

"I did too. They frightened me because in them I lose you. I never saw what chased you but knew it was your past, the secrets you kept. You wept for the dead men at your feet and I knew they were close to you. After meeting your unit I am pretty sure it was them." She shuddered remembering the tearing sense of loss each nightmare provoked.

He pulled her under his chin. "I could face anything but the deaths of my brothers," he whispered. He pulled back and looked her in the eye. "If I asked you to leave here with me, would you?"

She nodded without even needing to think about it. He was her mate and where he went, she would follow. "I would hope that before we leave you would trust me enough to tell me why you're so scared.

"I'm not scared," he protested immediately.

"I thought my mate was progressive enough and secure enough in his masculinity to admit to being afraid."

"It's technically not fear, it's an inborn sense of survival."

"Survival of what?"

"A massacre," he said softly.

"What massacre?" she asked.

"One that took place nearly five thousand years ago in Storm Keep."

"There was no massacre in Storm Keep," she scoffed.

"There was," he insisted.

"I think I would remember reading about that," she replied.

"There was," he repeated calmly.

"There wasn't!" she shouted, frightening herself. "Micah? What just happened?"

"That, my one and only, is a conditioned response that has been passed down at a genetic level based on a citywide manipulation of the people's memory." He pointed around to the darkened room and down to where they lay. "Most people react better in a dark, quiet room where they aren't distracted by what they see or hear. Physical contact also helps." He gave a low chuckle. "Yet another reason why I prefer you naked."

"There was a massacre?" she asked, afraid to believe her own mind.

"Yes. Storm Keep's royal family was driven from the castle and their most loyal retainers killed when the manipulation failed to work on them."

"The king and queen left," she corrected.

"Why? Where did they go?"

"They..." She shook her head back and forth trying to clear the haze.

"Shush, it's okay. It will be harder for you to fight the manipulation since you left Storm Keep this morning."

"What does that have to do with anything?"

"Whatever altered the memories of our people

five thousand years ago permeated the very stone of the castle turning it into a broadcast tower. The longer you are away from the city, the clearer your mind will become, it will also help if your memories are challenged on a regular basis."

"The people have the right to know," she started and he placed a finger on her lips. "Less than a dozen people know the truth. Any attempt to reveal what is going on will be shut down by innocent citizens. Remember your reaction."

"How do you know all this?"

He held her close. "My family served the Stormharts. The night it happened my great-grandparents were in the castle reporting to the king and queen."

"Reporting?"

He chuckled. "My family ran what would be equivalent to the intelligence service for the royal family back then. The Ashleighs were the sword, the Ironwoods the shield, but the Whiteoaks were the book."

"Whiteoaks?"

"My true last name, Whiteoak. Micah Whiteoak. My family is descended from the druidic line of the Darwids. Dar, means oak, wid roughly means to know. My people were scholars and seekers of knowledge. They used that knowledge to serve their king and queen."

"That's amazing."

"It was also a death sentence. Their minds were conditioned to question everything, to search out truths, and uncover secrets. None of the manipulation worked and they rose up to defend the king and queen. They're the ones who opened the way for them to escape. My grandmother lost everyone that night. Her parents, older brothers, uncles, aunts, the entire family gone, in eight blood filled hours."

"Oh your poor gran! How did she survive? How did she figure out what happened?" Serenity held him as he told his story.

"She badgered her parents into allowing her to train with the unit warriors. She wanted to hurry up and start field work. So she spent that weekend with the Nu unit. When she returned to the city and couldn't find her family she raced back to the units crying hysterically. They couldn't remember her family. To them, she had always been alone. Later she figured out that after she left the unit estate and was out of sight, the warriors' minds were altered," He took a shuddering breath. "The entire kingdom was gaslighted and my poor gran thought she was going mad. For the longest time she kept the truth to herself. She carved out a life and slowly began asking questions and gathering information. One by one she found other witches who had a different set of memories from what was generally accepted and they compiled all of what they learned into a book. One of those witches was in the castle that night and was able to tell my gran how bravely her family fought, but it was a cold comfort."

"What does that have to do with you now?" she failed to see how her mate could be in any danger. He didn't even have the same last name any more.

"I came here to Noctem Falls to investigate if a vampire or group of vampires could be responsible for the mass manipulation that happened that night. Because I am now the bearer of the Veritas

Book, the Book of Truth." He kissed the top of her head. "Our people are slaves to their own memories and I won't rest until the truth is known."

"Why not go to the Ironwoods or the Ashleighs? They're still around right?" She patched up Caiden just last week.

He shook his head. "One generation of their family was eliminated but a hundred years later they were back in the city as if nothing happened. I don't think they even remember their true purpose."

"Caiden, Tristan and Kyran Ironwood are good men. Law Ashleigh is a good man. If you helped them remember, they could stand by you." It scared her to death that her mate would face this future alone.

"It would take years to peel back that many layers of false memories and I don't think we have that much time."

"The ferals," she whispered.

"Reapers. Meryn called them reapers."

"You know what I mean."

"They are the larger threat right now so I want to stay with my unit brothers. But if my past is truly catching up with me, what I tell them could tear us apart. How could I look Adriel in the eye and confess that I have been lying to them for centuries. That I came here under false pretenses looking to discredit his people."

"I think he would forgive you and offer to help."

"I think you're being extremely optimistic."

"Do me a favor, at least tell Kendrick. He has had access to one of the largest collection of books in the kingdom for centuries. I know he could help," she pleaded.

He sighed. "If he wasn't an acting unit warrior I would say no. But technically he is a warrior brother and pretty much eschews all Storm Keep stands for. I'll feel him out, but make no promises."

"If I had to choose between an army or Kendrick at my side, I'd chose Kendrick every single time," she confessed.

He propped himself on his hand. "Do I need to feel jealous here?"

She shook her head. "No, he's..." she had to stop and think a moment. "He's sort of like an older brother, but not a kind, nice one like Zach. He's kinda sadistic and sarcastic as hell, but because he doesn't coddle you, he helps you to become stronger, to learn more and to push yourself." She exhaled. "There were times when I honestly wanted to choke him, but, I wouldn't be the witch I am today without his teasing, pointing, laughing and ridicule."

Micah frowned. "I don't need to beat his ass do I?"

"No, he was never malicious but I did provide entertainment for him more than once when studying for my Academy test."

He let out a nervous laugh. "Good, because have you seen the size of him? What did he eat growing up?"

"My family left Eiré Danu when we were about five so I could spend my formative years in Storm Keep and learn from other witches. Zach hung out with the fae warriors learning how to build muscle and how to fight. I got into scrapes with the other witch kids as we tried spells out on each other."

Micah chuckled. "I see that hasn't changed in the centuries since I grew up there."

"I wonder if I ever played on the same roads as you growing up? Or maybe passed your gran in the market?"

"We only missed each other by a century or two or three," he teased.

"A few centuries are nothing to paranormals."

"I'm glad we met when we did and not in Storm Keep," Micah said, kissing her forehead. "I was a cheeky shit until I hit three hundred. You would have hated me."

"I used to envy Laelia and Radclyffe, they've known since they were practically babies they were mates."

"How'd that happen?" he asked.

"They were born on the exact same, day, hour and minute. Radclyffe's family are very upper class. On the day he was born his mother went into labor while at the market, unfortunately for her, the closest assistance was the Water Temple in the Lower City. Laelia's parents were from the Lower City so of course when her mother went into labor she was brought to the Water Temple as well." She smiled as she remembered Radclyffe telling her the story excitedly as a child when they first met. "Anyway, both women were placed in the same birthing room. As the temple clock chimed midnight on All Hallows Eve, both babes drew breath and wailed," she giggled. "No one thought anything of it until about five years later. Radclyffe saw Laelia while he was at the market with his mother and followed Laelia home. Over the years Radclyffe was hauled back to his parents house by his ears nearly everyday. Laelia and I joke that his left ear is bigger than his right since his father is right-handed."

"You knew each other as children?" he asked.

"Yes, though when I returned to Storm Keep to study for my assessment and take over as head of the Water Temple it had been a while since I saw them. My family left Storm Keep right after Zach and I came of age.

"One of the first things I did when I returned to the city was look them up. They claimed one another not long after I left and moved to the Lower City to begin their work at the Water Temple."

"Why did neither of them become temple head?"

"Laelia said she didn't want the responsibility and Radclyffe was denied the position because his father is on the board that reviews applications for city positions. When they moved to the Lower City his family disowned him."

"Why the Water Temple?" he asked.

She smiled. "It's where they were born."

"I studied like a fiend and they would help me, though they avoided Kendrick like the plague," she gave a one shoulder shrug. "Everyone thinks I can fuss back at him because I'm not impressed by his power, but nothing could be further from the truth. Growing up I saw his immense power and it terrified me, but I knew if there was one person in all the world who could help me get stronger it was him. I wasn't fearless, I was stubborn," she swallowed hard. "And it helped that I saw how he was around Keelan."

"Were the two of you close?" Micah asked softly.

She nodded. "They didn't receive many guests considering Kendrick's sunny personality so Keelan got excited when I came to visit as a child. He was studying for his warrior exams and used to share his note taking techniques," she shuddered. "The entire city felt Kendrick's grief the night Keelan was lost."

"According to Meryn he's just not in his body right now," Micah clarified.

"What does that even mean?" she asked. The last update received from Kendrick while she was in Storm Keep was that he was working to help Keelan. When she offered to travel to Lycaonia to help he advised her it wasn't a medical issue and everything was being done to restore Keelan.

"I have no idea and the Alpha Unit is very 'hush hush' about it. Not because they don't trust us, but because whatever happened is so important that the fewer who know the details, the safer Keelan will be. All the warriors respect that decision and haven't pressed for more details."

"Maybe after we cure the virus we can help them," she suggested.

He smiled. "That sounds like a good plan to me." He gave her a quick kiss then closed his eyes. "We won't be able to help anyone if we don't get some sleep."

"I am hoping for sexy dreams with a montage of our claiming," she said before yawning.

"Me too," he said.

Before she could think of another topic to keep her wide awake his even breathing lulled her to sleep.

CHAPTER EIGHT

MICAH LEERED AT HIS MATE over coffee in their garden the next morning. "Thanks to your suggestion right before I nodded off, I dreamt about our claiming, it was a montage of sexy images, but done like an ESPN highlight reel." He sipped his coffee. "I got extra points for claiming you midair, then it got weird. We got stuck above the platform and my gran's next-door neighbor Mr. Compton had to get us down." He shook his head. "I don't know whether the dream was arousing, humiliating, or disturbing." He heard a thump and when he looked around he couldn't see his mate. Her cup of coffee was balanced precariously on the arm of the platform bed, but she was nowhere to be seen. "Serenity?" he called.

He heard a gasping noise under him and leaned over the side of the bed. His brilliant healer of a mate, had, once again, fallen over while laughing at him.

"Congratulations, I now have a complex," he chided.

"Micah, stop!" she yelled, while gales of laughter

echoed throughout his normally tranquil oasis.

He smiled at her antics. He loved how she gave herself over to her mirth and joy. She held nothing back when she laughed, he just wished it wasn't because she was laughing at him.

After a couple more minutes, she finally dragged herself back up on to the platform and took a sip of her coffee. "I needed that," she said, still smiling.

"I do aim to please." He leaned back. "What are our plans for the day?"

She looked at him funny. "Don't you have to patrol or do unit work? Back in Storm Keep the units were constantly running patrols around the city."

He shook his head. "Eta was assigned to Level One to rotate in guarding the mates." He grinned at her. "I'm your guard."

Behind them in the house the clock chimed and he stood. "Come on, my one and only. Time for breakfast." He rubbed his hands together. "I can't wait to see what Sebastian made, I hope we're having waffles, his waffles are legendary."

"So, everyone really does get together for meals?" She drained her coffee cup and followed him inside. "I hope Vivi has an update about Aiden's blood. As much as I would like to help in the lab all we can do as healers is make patients comfortable, we're useless when it comes to human science."

Micah took her cup and rinsed it out before putting it in the dishwasher. "That's why we take meals together. It's just easier to keep everyone on the same page. Not only is the food amazing but lately it's come to feel like home on Level One."

Micah couldn't wait to tease Radclyffe about his

ear. The witch had been giving him the evil eye ever since he announced Serenity was his mate. Maybe he'd slip it into conversation and see what happened.

"Why do you have an evil smirk?" his mate asked.

"Me?" he asked innocently.

She just shook her head. "Let's go, you have me craving waffles."

He walked over and took her hand. "Onward to waffles!" he announced pointing to the front door.

Serenity giggled and pointed. "Onward!"

Her mate was such a goofball, but she loved that about him. He made something as simple as heading to breakfast fun. When they arrived, Micah opened the door to the Rioux quarters. "Honey, we're home," he announced. They walked into the antechamber and closed the door behind them.

"In here darling," Declan replied in a falsetto voice.

Micah swung the dining room door open. "Did you miss me kitten?" he asked the lion shifter.

Declan chuckled. "Someone is in a fine mood," he arched a brow at them. Serenity blushed but Micah just gave his brother two thumbs up before sitting down next to her.

Aiden turned to Adriel. "You know, I think you do have it worse. At least I only have Colton to deal with."

Meryn shook her head. "And Sascha and Keelan

when he's better." She waved her fork at her mate. "Didn't you men install a freaking fireball alarm system at the Alpha estate."

Rheia nodded. "They had to confiscate the explosives from Graham."

Adriel's eyes were wide and he swallowed. "I think Declan and Micah are just fine."

"Oh yeah, we're fine," Micah said in a sultry voice.

Declan leaned back in his chair to give Micah a high five.

Adriel pinched the bridge of his nose. "Then again..."

Declan righted himself. "You invited us to live with you, you're stuck with us now," he reminded the unit leader.

Adriel gave them a satisfied smirk. "It also allows me to visit my godchildren more often." He looked over to Etain and gave a short nod.

Etain stood. "I do not mean to interrupt breakfast, but I have something important to announce." He looked down at Vivi who reached up and took his hand. "As you all know, Vivian and I are expecting our first child." Around the table everyone clapped and whistled. "What may not be more widely known is that we almost lost our daughter," his voice broke and he cleared his throat. The table quieted as the men frowned fiercely at the thought of something happening to one of their children. Etain continued. "We would have lost her, except my fae brothers here in the city contributed their light and gave her the strength to pull through. But they might not have made it in time had it not been for Micah."

Serenity turned to her mate who had a flush working up the back of his neck. "You saved her?" she asked softly.

Micah shook his head. "I just got help," he refuted. "The fae warriors did the saving."

Etain walked over to stand by their chairs. "You saved my daughter," he glanced over to Adriel who was grinning before looking down at Micah. "And I would be honored if you became her *athair*."

Micah's mouth dropped as he looked from Etain to Adriel to Declan and Grant. "That's not what we agreed on," he protested weakly.

Etain gave him a wicked grin. "I spoke with Adriel and he said he is looking forward to being an uncle to one of our children." His eyes softened. "Will you brother? Will you watch over my baby girl?"

Micah swallowed hard and kept blinking. Finally, he nodded and stood. "It would be an honor and a privilege to be *athair* to your daughter." They clasped forearms in a warrior shake before Etain pulled him into a hug. When they stepped back Micah still looked a bit dazed. Chuckling Etain gently pushed him back into his chair then sat back down.

"What a wonderful way to start the day," Magnus said smiling broadly.

"That was just beautiful," Sebastian said dabbing at his eyes with his towel. Hal sniffed loudly as he pushed the serving cart in from the kitchen. "My baby girl's baby girl now has an *athair*." He stopped beside Meryn. "Waffle?"

"Hell yeah," Meryn said holding up her plate.

Hal smiled and piled up a stack of waffles four

high. Meryn set her plate down. "Now that's what I'm talking about." She picked up one of the syrup dispensers and drenched her waffles.

Aiden looked at the growing amber puddle. "Maybe that's enough," he suggested.

"No. All the little squares have to have syrup," Meryn said turning her body slightly to protect her syrup.

"She's right Aiden," Micah agreed. "Each square needs its own pool of yummy goodness."

Grant shook his head reaching for the jam. "That's way too sweet for me."

"What do I do?" Pip asked Aiden looking from the syrup to the jam. Serenity noticed that although Pip adored Meryn, he looked to Aiden for advice and protection.

Aiden thought for a moment. "Try just a little bit of syrup and if you like it you can always add more," he suggested.

"Caiden sings your praises all the time saying how strict and diligent you are in training and creating drills. But you're kind as well," Serenity said complimenting the large commander.

Aiden shrugged. "He reminds me of Ben when he was younger."

Micah blinked. "I keep forgetting you have a younger brother."

Rex smiled. "Younger brothers are one of life's biggest joys and the biggest pains in the ass you can experience."

Aiden, Kendrick, Magnus, and Etain nodded solemnly. Declan rolled his eyes. "Older brothers are great for being there when you need help," he eyed Rex. "Whether you ask for it or not."

Again, Aiden nodded, this time along with Rheia, Caspian and Serenity.

Laelia looked to the unit commander. "You have three brothers, don't you?"

Aiden nodded. "Two older and one younger."

Laelia looked impressed. "Your family is truly blessed."

He smiled. "I think the true blessings are my parents."

"They are relatively close in age too," Declan pointed out.

Rex nodded. "Having a lot of siblings is getting rarer these days."

Etain chuckled. "You never know. My parents surprised me with a set of twin siblings when I was a thousand years old. I went from being an only child to having a brother and a sister."

Meryn took a huge swig of coffee. "Y'all will have it easy with three squires. I mean, they could rotate babysitting duties and still run all three households."

Hal and Sebastian paused in their serving and looked at each other. Hal grinned. "Well now."

Sebastian nodded. "Well now, indeed."

"I can create a schedule and rotations," Kari offered. "I will be grateful for any help you can provide."

Rex tapped his chin. "We can interview for a squire for your household. Lionhart is a Founding Family after all."

Sebastian frowned. "That would mean we would get less time with the baby," he argued, then shook his head. "No. Hal, Pavil and myself are more than enough for Level One." He inclined his head to

Ryuu. "And, of course, Ryuu when little Meryn visits."

Magnus cut up his waffles. "The boss has spoken," he said. Kari then Beth began to chuckle. Magnus shrugged. "It is okay my dears, we all know Sebastian runs Level One."

Sebastian flailed his tea towel about Magnus' head. "I do not!" Magnus just stared out at the table as the tea towel bounced off of him.

Aiden nodded. "Marius ran our house growing up and I'm pretty sure Ryuu will be the only thing keeping us alive after the babies are born."

Ryuu gave a modest shrug. "Every house gets a bit chaotic when a baby arrives."

Kari sighed. "I am not looking forward to doing all the laundry."

Sebastian moved away from Magnus. "Do not worry I will be there to help." He dismissed Magnus with a hand wave. "I am sure Magnus can manage making his own meals a few nights a week."

Magnus stopped chewing. "What now?"

Kari stared up at Sebastian with huge eyes. "You would help us that much?"

"Of course! And I will babysit whenever you need me," he offered.

Magnus rubbed his chin in thought. "I do enjoy cooking shows," he admitted.

Broderick looked at Magnus in horror before turning to Rex. "I think a Lionhart squire is a wonderful idea."

Magnus looked offended. "This could be a great opportunity. I do not even know what the kitchen really looks like or how things are laid out. I may have to change things a bit."

Sebastian's smile faltered. "What?"

Magnus looked over to his brother. "We could try new dishes together." He turned back to Meryn. "Meryn, can you be a dear and look up the recipe for that dessert where you use a mini flame thrower," he asked excitedly.

Sebastian paled. "I am sure I can manage our kitchen and helping Kari, you do not need to cook Magnus," he backtracked quickly.

Meryn's fingers were already moving. "Magnus will you buy me a real flame thrower."

"Of course, dear," Magnus answered.

"See! That! That right there!" Aiden exclaimed. "We need parameters."

Meryn stuck her tongue out at her mate. "He already said yes."

Sebastian wiped his hands on his towel. "I will ask Pavil if he knows of any squires who he trusts to move down to Level One. We can conduct interviews after the virus is cured."

"But..." Magnus protested looking crushed.

Sebastian shook his head. "Stay out of my kitchen." He looked around the table. "Looks like we are out of coffee. Be right back." He hurried through the doors to the kitchen.

The moment the door closed Meryn's fingers stilled and she put her laptop away beside her chair. She and Magnus exchanged winks.

Beth gasped. "You..." she covered her mouth with her hands and looked around making sure Sebastian couldn't hear her.

Magnus took a sip of his juice. "What a truly amazing morning," he said to no one in particular. He looked over to Kari. "I think getting you a squire is an excellent idea. Babies are a lot of work and you will need someone you can rely on around the clock to assist you."

Sebastian slunk back into the dining room looking defeated. "I still want to help babysit," he said quietly, holding a carafe of coffee to his chest.

Kari stood and hurried over to the squire. "Of course, you can! In fact, I will not take on any squire unless you approve of them. They must pass every test you can think of. Getting someone you recommend is the second-best thing to having your help. I trust you implicitly."

Sebastian looked overwhelmed. "It would be an honor to help." He kissed her forehead and she walked back to her chair. He glared at Magnus. "That was mean."

Magnus shrugged. "You will be busy arranging things for our Bethy even after she returns to Lycaonia, do not be greedy and try to monopolize all the babies."

"That is true, I already have things on backorder for her." He reached down and plucked at Magnus' sleeve. "And you need an entirely new wardrobe," Sebastian said staring at Magnus' rolled up cuffs again.

Magnus eyed his shirt in disgust. "I could understand if I gained height like Gavriel or even noticeable bulk like our commander here," he said pointing to Aiden. "But to only grow enough so that none of my clothes fit is ridiculous." He blushed slightly. "I will not even go into how my underthings chafe."

"You should totally wear sweats and free ball it," Meryn suggested.

Magnus' eyes narrowed. "Does that mean what I think it means?"

Around the table the men nodded and a chorus of 'yeses' sounded off.

Sebastian shuddered. "Just. No."

Gavriel nodded in sympathy to Magnus' plight. "Do not remind me. It took months to replace all my leather."

Beth lowered her fork. "What leather? I've never seen you in leather before."

Gavriel turned to his mate. "Before our uniforms were designed to mimic the human military, most units wore leather pants, vests and jackets. It is a long-lasting material and can be hardened to act as light armor."

Beth's eyes traveled down his body. "Hmmm."

"Beth!" Gavriel exclaimed, looking shocked.

Caspian hid a smile behind his napkin. "I have days when I wonder how much I influenced Bethy growing up, then we have moments like this and I am like, "oh, there I am"."

"Y'all are leather daddies!" Meryn declared, her eyes wide. She reached down and pulled her phone out of her bag.

Around the table Rex, Law and Grant spit out the juice they had just sipped. Rheia pounded on Colton's back, as he choked, while he tried to stop laughing long enough to breathe.

Aiden looked down at his mate. "Do you know what that means?"

"Yeah, it means that y'all wear leather." She gave him an exasperated look. "My furries talk about leather daddies all the time. And bears." Her face grew thoughtful. "I didn't think that many of them were bear-shifters though."

Aiden snapped his mouth closed and took a deep breath. "Pass the syrup," he said, pointing to the dispenser. Meryn handed it to him and turned back to her waffles while she checked her phone one handedly.

Declan stared at him in awe. "I think he just deleted that from his memory."

Grant nodded like that made sense. "I think that's how he survives."

"Wait until my furries find out y'all are leather daddies," Meryn said her thumb moving a mile a minute.

Without even looking up from his waffles Aiden simply plucked her phone from her hand and threw it up in the air behind them. Ryuu caught it easily and tucked it away in his jacket.

"Rude!" Meryn bellowed. Aiden continued eating his waffles.

"Good job Aiden," Beth said in admiration.

Aiden glanced down the table at her and winked. He shoved another two waffles in his mouth and reached for his coffee.

Grant turned to Declan. "We are in the presence of a master."

Meryn pulled her laptop back out. "Okay, so obviously if I am banned from Facebook then I misunderstood what a leather daddy was."

Aiden eyed her closely. "What are you going to do?"

"Google it," she replied.

"No Facebook," he warned.

"No Facebook," she agreed.

"I'm spending the day with Kari and uncle,"

Beth said quickly.

"Vivi and I will be in the lab," Rheia added.

Anne turned to Ellie. "We'll be busy on Level Six with the children."

"I'll be in meetings with Stefan all morning," Eva added.

Serenity watched as the women effectively called 'not it' in response to Meryn's sudden thirst for learning.

Micah turned to her and raised a brow. She nodded. Someone had to watch over the odd human and if she were completely honest with herself, she was dying to see what she said next.

"My one and only and I can keep the midget company today," Micah offered magnanimously.

Around the table the men exhaled in relief. Serenity could tell that each of them envisioned fielding questions from Meryn all morning about different lifestyles choices.

"I'm not a midget," Meryn protested sounding distracted. She tilted her head sideways to look at her laptop.

Aiden looked over at them. "You have my thanks."

Serenity turned to Ryuu. "Can you watch over her later, so I can do rounds up at the hospital."

Ryuu nodded. "Of course. Let me know whenever you need to leave, looking after Meryn is no hardship." Serenity had a feeling there wasn't much Ryuu would consider a hardship.

Serenity turned to Vivi. "Did you make any headway with Aiden's blood yesterday?"

Vivi nodded. "Thanks to Kendrick we can see the virus now to run different tests. We found out that whoever created this thing based it on Hepatitis C, which is why the warriors were immune, they all received the vaccine for it. I'm trying to backward engineer a cure based on that, but it's going to take a while."

Colton frowned. "Can't you just give them the vaccine?"

Ellie shook her head. "A vaccine is a preventative measure not a medicine," she said sounding sad.

"We are a step closer than we were yesterday," Adriel reminded them.

Vivi brightened. "You're absolutely right. We're light years ahead of where we were even earlier this week."

Kari held up her iPad. "Do not forget we have the meeting with the Founding Family and Noble Heads this afternoon to update everyone concerning Warrick's elevation in rank and to let them know Magnus is cured."

Around the table groans went up. Kari ignored them. "Personally, I am looking forward to it. These changes are a long time coming," she said, grinning evilly.

Magnus sat back. "I find that I am looking forward to it as well," he admitted.

Meryn picked up her laptop and rotated it ninety degrees. Magnus frowned. "Meryn, what is the matter?"

"Do you think naked men look weird? I mean, the gods or whoever were on the right track creating man. Chest muscles, forearms, chiseled eight pack and then. Bam! Penis, kinda stuck on like an afterthought." She turned her laptop again. "Looks detachable."

Aiden's head snapped around. "What are you looking at!" He grabbed her laptop, shut it and handed it to Ryuu.

"I'm studying art!" Meryn protested.

"Naked art?" Aiden asked. "How did you go from leather daddies to naked art?"

Meryn blinked. "I don't know. I just kept clicking links and before I knew it..."

Rheia gave Meryn a sympathetic looked. "I've done something like that before. I Googled homeschooling curriculums for Penny, which led me to this site about homesteading, then canning, then disaster prepping. I logged off when I realized I had spent an hour reading about cult suicides."

Aiden paled. "The Google is dangerous?"

"That happens to me all the time, it's how I learn," Meryn said. "But usually it's about blood splatter, serial killers and corpse farms."

Declan leaned forward. "What on earth is a corpse farm?"

Meryn's face lit up. "It's where research facilities put out a whole bunch of dead bodies in like a field with cages around them, so scavengers can't get to them and they study stuff like rate of decomposition and how long it takes for bugs to get in the body, and maggot growth, stuff like that."

Aiden spit out his waffles and covered his mouth with his hand. Serenity heard dry heaves and saw that Colton was hanging on by a thread. Laelia popped up out of her seat and placed a hand on his back. Serenity sent soothing magic around the table to settle the more delicate tummies.

Sebastian sighed. "Now that breakfast is over, I will bring in extra coffee, lattes and espressos to fortify everyone for their day."

Ryuu patted Meryn on the head and looked around the room. "Isn't she adorable?"

Colton looked up at Aiden a bit wild eyed. "Thank the gods Keelan wasn't here for that." Aiden nodded.

Meryn squirted ketchup all over her scrambled eggs. Colton and surprisingly Rex bolted from the room. Meryn chuckled and kept eating. Laelia shook her head and sat back down. Radclyffe rubbed her back. "You tried, dearest."

"Adorable," Ryuu repeated.

Kendrick chuckled. "That she is."

"Thank god the twins weren't here," Rheia said leaning back in her chair as Hal started picking up plates.

Serenity watched as Meryn got really interested in her eggs. She wasn't the only one who noticed.

Aiden leaned in. "What are they doing Meryn?"

"Hmmm?" she looked up at him eyes wide.

"Meryn," he growled.

"It wasn't my idea," she started.

"What wasn't your idea?"

She took a deep breath, then hesitated. "Do you *really*, really want to know? I mean later you won't be lying when you tell the council you had no idea what was going on."

Aiden's eyes bugged out. "What in the gods' names are they doing?"

"Wellllll," Meryn dragged out the word.

When Aiden fumbled at his waist for his walkie-talkie she grabbed it and started talking fast. "The twins and I didn't like how DeLaFontaine hurt Pip so much. And he's our brother now, so we're sort of legally obligated to defend him and make sure that it never happens again."

Pip's eyes filled. "They are doing something for me?"

Meryn turned in her chair to face him. "Yup. Your bio-dad did very bad things that hurt a lot of people, but one of the worst things he did was mistreat you.

"Your parents and guardians are supposed to take care of you and feed you and make you feel safe and teach you how to make your way in the world. But he didn't do any of those things and he hurt you. He will eventually pay for his crimes against the city and her people, we just wanted to make sure that he paid for what he did to you too."

Aiden sat back. "I can't even get mad over that. I'm sure whatever you do will be worth whatever lecture the council comes up with."

Magnus cleared his throat. "Part of the council is sitting right here." Meryn gulped, and he continued. "Considering the severity of his other crimes I cannot see you getting *too* stern of a lecture." He eyed her closely. "What did you do?"

Meryn beamed. "Diarrhea."

Magnus turned to Ryuu. "Simply adorable."

CHAPTER NINE

SERENITY AND HER MATE, WITH Meryn and Pip in tow, caught up to the twins in Meryn's bat cave. Meryn rushed over to them. "Did it work?" she asked, as they crowded around a monitor.

Nigel nodded. "We think so. Though, we forgot the guy who attacked Kari and Jervasius Régis was still down there, so they may have gotten it too."

Meryn shrugged. "Serves them right."

Serenity leaned over Meryn's shoulder to watch what looked to be closed circuit video. "Is there sound?" she asked as she watched DeLaFontaine throw an epic temper tantrum. The other prisoner was already doubled over on his toilet.

Neil laughed. "Yeah, but we have the volume turned down. He's cussing a lot and making death threats. Opps!" he pointed to the monitor as DeLa-Fontaine raced to the corner fumbling with his pants. He turned to Meryn. "Building in anger as a trigger was genius."

"Ut oh," Nigel whispered as they watched Leif and Travis walk in. They had only taken two steps when both covered their mouths and started gagging.

Neil's eyes were huge as they watched the two unit warriors back out of the cells. "They must have gone in because DeLaFontaine started shouting. They are gonna kill us, they have guard duty down there this week."

Meryn snickered. "Stay close to Kendrick," she advised.

Serenity turned to Pip who had watched everything quietly. "Pip are you okay?"

Meryn and the boys turned to glance behind them where Pip stood off to one side. Neil looked worried. "Did we go too far?" he asked.

Pip took a few steps closer. "He looks so small on your screen." His hand reached out to touch the monitor. "Was he always so..."

"Flawed?" Meryn asked supplying the word. Pip nodded. Meryn bumped hips with him. "I think he looks smaller to you because your world got bigger."

Pip looked at her frowning. "Why did I want his approval so much?"

Meryn turned back to the screen. "Because he is your dad, and no matter how awful they are, we always want the approval of our family."

Pip straightened his back. "He is not my family. Not anymore."

Neil slung an arm around his shoulder. "You have us now. We're still learning a lot ourselves, but maybe that's why we can help you more. The warriors have forgotten what it's like growing up in our world."

Pip brightened. "Can you help me fly better? I

still wobble."

The twins grinned at each other and Nigel nodded. "We sure can. If you can wait a bit, we're compiling all the video footage we gathered from the Pits for Meryn. After that we can go with you. You don't have to worry about falling with us there. You can practice all you want."

Neil looked over to Meryn. "You want to come with us?"

She shook her head. "I'm going with Serenity and Micah when they look in on the kiddos. Then after that we have to come back down to Level One for a boring ass bigwig meeting."

Serenity eyed Meryn. "I didn't know you wanted to check on the children."

Meryn blinked at her. "I don't. But I'll tag along so I can visit Mr. Culpepper and Old Man Richter on Level Six so they can feed me."

Serenity stared back at Meryn. "You don't care about the children?"

Meryn shrugged. "I don't know them, or their parents. I'm not a nurse and I kinda don't like kids in general. Penny is the exception because she's a Whovian."

"But you're pregnant," Serenity pointed out.

Meryn looked down at her belly in surprise. "I am?? How'd that happen?" she asked sarcastically.

"You know what I mean," Serenity said gently bopping her on the nose.

Meryn's scrunched up her face and rubbed her nose. "Aiden wanted an ankle biter. Besides I think my kid is going to be kick ass, so of course I'm going to love him or her."

Pip smiled at Meryn shyly. "I think you will an

amazing mother." The twins nodded their agreement and Meryn blushed furiously. "Beth said I just gotta make sure they aren't starving, hurt or rocking themselves in a corner. That doesn't sound too hard and I'll have Ryuu with me."

Micah ruffled her short brown hair. "You can do it, my delicate little flower."

She smiled up at him. "I love your nicknames. At home they just call me Menace. Yours are nicer."

Micah swept his hand to his chest. "Don't hate them because they aren't me," he said in a tragic tone.

Serenity crossed her leg in front of her and gently kicked the inside of Micah's knee making him wobble. The twins laughed, and Micah turned his head to wink at her.

"Goofball," she said warmly.

"Your goofball," he corrected.

"Told you he was nice," Meryn pointed out.

Serenity smiled at her. "You did, and you were right. Fate gave me the most perfect mate in the whole world."

Micah straightened and pulled her into his arms so that her back was flush against his chest. He wrapped his arms loosely about her waist. "I'm the lucky one."

"Awww y'all are so cute," Meryn said looking happy for them.

"Meryn, if you want time to eat you better head up now," Neil said pointing to the time on the monitor. "I know how you can get to talking with Mr. Culpepper."

Micah pulled his walkie-talkie from his waist. "Ryuu, we're heading up to Level Six with the midget."

A moment later Ryuu responded. "One moment, I am on my way."

Meryn tilted her head. "Why'd you call him if you're my guard?"

Micah reattached his walkie-talkie. "Because that man isn't skinning me alive on the off chance something was to happen to you. If it were just you and I going I may not have called him. But since my one and only is coming with us, I know my focus will be on her."

"You have no idea how happy I am to hear you admit such a thing," Ryuu said, walking through the door. "It eases my mind knowing that you take such things into consideration when you are guarding my *denka*."

Micah grinned impishly. "And I don't want to end up electrocuted by blue light."

Ryuu's mouth twitched. "And there's that."

Meryn turned to the boys. "Y'all have fun and make sure the net is in place before you practice with Pip."

"Yes, Meryn," the twins said in unison.

Meryn stepped beside Ryuu. "Let's go get some food."

Serenity took Micah's hand. "And check on the children."

Meryn shrugged. "Yeah, them too."

When they got to Level Six Meryn surprisingly

stayed with them as they headed toward the hospital.

"I thought you didn't like kids?" Micah asked.

"Doesn't mean I want them sick either. Maybe I can fluff pillows or something."

When they walked into the hospital Ryuu immediately took a protective stance in front of Meryn. All around them the kids were thrashing, hissing and attacking their guardians.

Serenity turned to Ryuu. "Get her out of here. We'll meet you by that vendor she likes." Ryuu simply nodded and steered Meryn back out the door. The second they were gone Serenity and Micah sprinted to different beds to help the parents.

Behind her she heard both Hawthorne, Kendrick and Micah casting the *Immobiles* spell in an effort to get the children secured. Serenity immediately went to Ellie. "What can I do?" she asked as she approached.

Ellie was struggling to pin the arms down to one of the girls. "Anything you can to calm them down!" Ellie shouted.

Serenity looked around the room. Laelia had already extended her magic on the left side of the room and Radclyffe on the right. Instead of trying to reach each child she used her best friends as conduits and began send her power into them.

In her minds eyes she concentrated on activating the parts of the brain that regulated sleep. She gradually started increasing the melatonin levels. "*Dormite, dormite, dormite,*" she whispered urging them to sleep.

It took over ten minutes of concentrating on

regulating her power flow before a hand caressed her shoulder.

"They're asleep, my one and only," Micah said softly.

As she pulled back the last bit of her power her knees buckled and she was swept up in her mate's arms.

"We're heading to the Culpepper stand," Micah whispered.

Serenity struggled to keep her eyes open. "Laelia, Radclyffe?"

"We're here," said a soft voice at her side. Serenity turned her head and smiled at her friends. Laelia's face looked pale but otherwise she seemed fine. "Thank the gods you came when you did. We just finished up their snacks when they started to get out of control."

"Your power?" Serenity asked.

Laelia shook her head. "Doing better than yours."

Rheia hurried over. "Is she alright?"

Serenity nodded. "Just knackered."

Rheia looked over her shoulder at the room. "How long do we have before they wake?"

Serenity yawned. "Twelve to fifteen hours for sure. If you don't have catheters in, you may want to tell the parents to get them in diapers."

Rheia chewed on her lower lip. "Can you guarantee me they will be out for at least twelve hours?"

Laelia placed a comforting hand on Rheia's shoulder. "If Serenity said twelve it will be twelve, at the very least. I'd be surprised if the kids wake up again before breakfast tomorrow. Right now, they are sleeping better than anyone in the city. Serenity pumped them full of melatonin."

·

Rheia exhaled. "I'm going to get the parents to diaper the kids then see if we can coax them to get some sleep. The twins widened the alcoves the beds are in to accommodate the visitor chair beds, it's time they were put to use. We'll rotate nursing duties to keep the kids clean and comfortable." She turned to Laelia and Radclyffe. "You two are off duty. You are essentially our only form of medicine. Go home, sleep, relax and recharge. Doctor's orders."

Marjoram walked over to Rheia and pointed to the door. "I'll take care of the parents. I'm sending you girls down to Level One for some rest. We'll all catch up in the antechamber before dinner."

Ellie and Anne walked up with their mates. Anne wrapped an arm around Rheia. "We're heading down now. Kendrick and I will be attending the Level One meeting so you and Ellie can get some rest. If anything crazy happens, I'll tell you all about it."

Serenity looked up at Micah. "We need to go get Meryn."

Kendrick's eyes darted around the room. "She's not here, is she?"

Micah shook his head. "No we sent her Mr. Culpepper's stand the second we saw what was happening."

Kendrick's eyes widened. "Alone?"

Serenity snorted. "Of course not, she has her squire with her."

Kendrick looked relieved. "Let's go collect our midget and head to Level One."

Serenity thought about asking Micah to put her down, but she was really comfortable. She closed her eyes and rested her cheek on his shoulder.

Micah ran his lips back and forth on her fore-head before kissing her. "As soon as we get Meryn we'll head back to my place."

Serenity sighed. "As much as I want to go relax in your garden, I think we should go to that meet-ing then check on Vivi. She's pregnant too and the stress has to be getting to her."

Micah's eyes were filled with worry. "You expended a lot of magic getting these kids to sleep. You need your rest."

"I can rest during the meeting. I'm not present-ing or anything. I just want to listen." She leaned closer. "I can also tell when heart rates change or if people start sweating. Gavriel and Magnus may need feedback later."

Micah snuggled her close. "Between you and Meryn any guilty parties don't stand a chance."

"What do you mean?"

He winked. "Tell you downstairs."

"Meryn, come on," Rheia called as they walked up to the vendor's stand.

Meryn's head popped out from behind the can-vas flap. "Are the kids done being bat shit crazy?"

Rheia covered her face with her palm. "Oh, Meryn," she murmured.

Meryn walked out with Ryuu behind her. "What? Tell me what I saw in there wasn't a prime example of bat shit crazy."

Kendrick could only nod. "You are absolutely correct Meryn. Now, come on. It's time to go be entertained by the Level One meeting."

Meryn's eyes lit up. "Sweet!"

Rheia looked over to Serenity. "Politics is like

one big game to them."

Kendrick raised a brow. "One we're very good at."

Rheia yawned. "Well I'm skipping this one. I know Kari will have the entire thing transcribed, in triplicate and color coded by dinner so I'll catch the highlights then."

Ellie smiled. "You're right, she will. I don't feel so bad about skipping it myself."

Grant nuzzled her neck. "You need to rest. You were with the kids all morning. We'll leave Benji with Adora a bit longer and take a nap."

Laelia and Radclyffe waved and headed toward the guest house they were staying at with Marjoram. The rest made their way to the tunnel and separated once they got to Level One. Ellie and Grant waved and kept walking toward the Ambrosios quarters. Rheia went inside the Rioux quarters heading toward their guest rooms while everyone else veered left toward the meeting room.

Right outside the doorway Micah gently set her on her feet. "I wish I could hold you all day."

"Your arms would fall off," she joked as they walked in and took the seats reserved for them in the front. Around the entire perimeter of the room unit warriors stood, their feet slightly apart and their hands clasped behind them. Instead of sitting next to his mate, Aiden stood by the stage looking out at the crowd.

She turned back to her mate and she leaned closer. "What were you going to tell me about Meryn?" she whispered.

Micah said a quick soundproof spell. "Not many people know, but she is empathic. She can read emotions and can usually tell when someone is lying."

Serenity turned and stared at the small human who was talking with Anne and Kendrick. "That odd duck is empathic? The one who didn't really care if the kids were sick? That human?"

Micah chuckled. "Don't hold her honesty against her. She had a rough childhood, so she never really learned how to trust others. She is getting better though. When she first got here she barely let us ruffle her hair. And you saw her at dinner the other night, she willingly gave Pip a hug."

"If anyone needs hugs, it's Pip. That poor young man has been through hell," Serenity said, thinking of the adorable vampire.

Micah shook his head. "If anyone needs a hug, it's Meryn." His eyes were serious for a change. "Why do you think she understands Pip?"

Serenity turned back to really look at Meryn. It was true that the woman was outlandish, nuts, and generally disliked people in general, but there was no denying the depth of emotion she exhibited when she was telling Pip why they felt the need to punish DeLaFontaine. "She's so little," Serenity said. "There's so much to her, it's hard to imagine it's all crammed in her tiny neurotic body."

Micah laughed. "You haven't seen neurotic yet. We'll skip coffee at our house tomorrow and go right to Level One. Meryn without coffee is a show."

Serenity was about to respond when Kari approached the podium. Gavriel and Adriel sat in two of the three empty chairs on the stage. Micah lowered their soundproof spell.

Kari tapped on the mic. "Can I have quiet please?" Around them the murmurs died off immediately. "Thank you."

Slowly Serenity sent out her magic so it barely touched those in attendance. She kept it at a low-level hum so no one would notice it. Or so she thought. Meryn turned in her chair to frown at her. Serenity shook her head and Meryn nodded, then gave Kari her full attention.

"Thank you all for coming on such short notice. We have a lot to go over, so I want to get started immediately." She tapped on her iPad on the podium. "Our first order of business is to..."

Hugo Evreux stood. "No offense to you Ms. Kari, but why is the prince not the one present-ing?"

Gavriel stood and simply projected his voice. "Please do not make me present. I am nowhere near as organized as she is," he said in an urbane manner.

Around the room everyone chuckled. Hugo nodded. "She is prettier too," he said winking up at Kari before sitting down.

Beside her she watched Meryn tilt her head then lean in toward Kendrick. "See, he's not a douche-bag. Maybe it's not genetic."

The entire room turned to stare at her and her cheeks blazed bright red. "Right. Paranormal hear-ing, still learning that one obviously." Guffaws took over. On the stage Gavriel turned around and his shoulders were shaking. Kari on the other hand looked mortified. Meryn mouthed, 'I'm sorry'. Kari gave her a weak smile, took a sip of water and cleared her throat. Beside her Gavriel sat back down, though he tried to look stern, his mouth was twitching horribly. "In keeping with the buoyant atmosphere, I am happy to announce that Prince Magnus has made a full recovery and may be joining us soon."

Serenity felt a huge tug on her magic and looked down the row. Though clapping with everyone else, this man's heart rate had skyrocketed. Meryn followed her line of sight. She squinted, then turned to look at her. She opened her mouth to say something then pulled out her phone. She typed something, then handed it to her. Serenity felt her breath catch when she saw the words typed in the notepad.

Hatred, confusion, rage. Lots of red slashes and streaks of black oil.

She passed the phone back to Meryn and continued to monitor the room.

Javier stood. "That is wonderful news Kari! What is delaying him?"

Kari frowned. "Unfortunately, that has to do with the bit of bad news I had to share. The children took another turn for the worse, he is being briefed by one of the doctors now."

Instantly she felt a jolt of satisfaction from the man.

Under her breath she heard Meryn whisper, "asshole,". Luckily everyone else had started speaking lowly at Kari's announcement so they didn't hear her.

Javier sat back down when Kari raised her hand for silence once more. "Thank you. Even though Prince Magnus has recovered, Prince Gavriel is still heading up the multiple investigations regarding this mysterious virus and other crimes against our people." She heaved a great sigh. "It is with a heavy heart that I confirm what some of you may have heard already as rumor. Ivan DeLaFontaine and Jervasius Régis have been arrested and are currently being held in the detention cells."

Around them everyone began speaking at once. Questions were shouted at Kari and arguments broke out around the room. Gavriel stood his face dark. "Quiet," he said, in a low, but stern voice. When everyone fell silent, he continued. "There is another reason you do not want me presenting," his eyes bled crimson and nearly everyone instinctively scooted back. "I am barely keeping my anger in check. Recent information given to me, coupled with hearing those two traitors' names again, has put me in the foulest mood I have been in, in centuries." He took a deep breath. "We will continue the meeting but please understand this is mostly a one-way communication. Kari will update you, advise you of new changes, then close the meeting. I am neither looking for feedback nor seeking permission for what we will do." He turned to Kari. "Please continue."

Kari gave a short nod. "As I was saying. DeLaFontaine was caught in the act of trying to inject Princess Vivian with a pure strain of the virus. He is being questioned as our lead suspect in the murder of Clara Garcia. Future charges are pending as the virus spreads and gets worse." She tapped her iPad. "Jervasius Régis was arrested for kidnapping, false imprisonment, sexual assault and frankly too many other disgusting things to mention." She looked out at the crowd. "He forced Bree to be his wife, I refuse to use the term mate, since he knew that her true mate was their squire Pavil Desrosiers. She lived with him against her will as Jervasius threatened to kill Pavil if she left." Gasps were heard all around them. Kari continued. "Prince Gavriel sees this as a serious betrayal of all we hold sacred. Jervasius will face a tribunal as soon as all the Elders are able to return to the city." She straightened her back. "This left our leaders with some serious decisions to make. Jervasius will of course be replaced by his son Jourdain as the new Régis Founding Family head." She paused as Jourdain stood and got a brief round of applause. No one looked surprised, he was the obvious choice. Kari clapped exactly twice then resumed her announcement. "As DeLaFontaine has no documented heir, Princes Gavriel, Adriel and Caspian, along with Princess Vivian and later Prince Magnus have all agreed, that given the disturbing reports from Level Five, it is their unanimous decision to elevate one of our Noble Family sons to serve as Level Five's new Founding Family head." Heads turned as those around them tried to figure out who could possibly be chosen for such a prestigious advancement. Kari smiled warmly. "It is with great honor I present to you, for the first time, our newest Founding Family head, Warrick Fortier." Warrick stepped away from the wall where he had been standing with his fellow unit warriors and walked in front of the stage.

The man who had seemed so triumphant at the children's distress stood to his feet. "Impossible!" he shouted.

Warrick's icy gaze turned to the man. "Uncle. Thank you for standing. It made locating you in the crowd that much easier." He turned to Viktor. "Could the Iota Unit please secure Gerald and Andre Dubois and take them to the detention cells for questioning?"

Viktor turned an evil grin to the frozen Gerald. "With pleasure."

Gerald attempted to run but Hugo stretched out a long leg and tripped him. Another man stopped Andre from bolting and the warriors escorted them out of the room. Warrick turned back to the crowd. "I know there have been so many changes lately. Trust me, I was not expecting this," he rubbed the back of his neck.

"Go on son," Hugo called out.

Warrick nodded. "I know many of you from attending functions with my uncle, I hope that by now you know me to be an honest man and a proud warrior for my city. I am asking for your trust now." He pointed to the door his uncle had just been dragged through. "I cannot divulge why they are being arrested, but I can tell you that I have recently discovered that they are responsible for harming many innocent citizens on Level Five. These crimes are so heinous and encompass so many from the Noble Family that I have asked Prince Gavriel dissolve the house completely. At this time, we have no future plans for the house."

"Prince Gavriel," a man called out, rising to his feet. "We mean no disrespect to you, but what is being discussed affects families who have ruled for generations. Was there nothing else that could be done?" he asked in soft, even tones.

Gavriel shook his head. "I know these measures seem extreme to you, but I will call on your trust

as Warrick has. I am desperately trying to save this
city, and I do not mean from the threat the virus
holds. Something darker has taken root in this city
and it is spreading like a cancer. What you see as
changes to established families, I see as precise surgery to remove the sickness that if left alone will
destroy our city."

Serenity could feel the effect Gavriel's words had
on the crowd. Nearly everyone was shaking from
the dire message the prince shared. There were no
pulses of adrenaline. She turned to Meryn who
was already passing her her phone.

Fear, gratitude, hope. Scared shitless, but good vibes.

Serenity nodded. That matched the reactions she
was feeling. She passed the phone back to Meryn.
She looked to the stage and saw Kari was watching
them closely. Serenity met her eye then gave a sub-
tle, slow nod. Kari's was about to continue when
her eyes widened. Serenity turned her head to see
what she was staring at.

Meryn stood and was raising her hand. Kari
looked positively ill. "Yes? Meryn."

Once again Meryn found herself the center
of attention. She looked a bit spooked but took
a deep breath. "Uh, your princes," she started.
Gavriel stood and walked closer to the edge of the
stage. "Just speak like you normally would," he said
kindly.

Kari coved the mic with her hand. "Are you
crazy?" she demanded. Like Meryn, she had also
forgotten about paranormal hearing.

The tension in the room dropped significantly as
chuckles erupted. "Oh, let the little one speak her
mind Ms. Kari," Hugo said, his eyes sparkling. "But

maybe move her on stage so we can see her."

Meryn grinned at him. "I knew I liked him," she said, then climbed onto her chair. Kendrick stood and placed a steadying hand on her back. Meryn looked around the room. "Okay peeps, I'm not from here, but I've met a lot of cool people since I've arrived, most of them being like *real* people on Level Six." On stage Kari groaned at the term 'real people'. Meryn ignored her. "Anyway. Since Warrick is a unit warrior and used to doing patrols and rounds and talking to different people on different levels. Instead of doing another Noble Family, why not create a mini-citizen council who can collect concerns from the people and present them to Warrick for action. He can either address the concerns directly or because he is now a Founding Family peep, he can bring it to a meeting like this?"

After she finished there was silence. Meryn looked around nervously. "It was just a thought." Kendrick helped her step down and she sat quickly.

Gavriel continued to stare for a moment more before he gracefully jumped from the stage. When he reached Meryn, he knelt down on one knee, and took her hand in his. "As always you seem to see the clearest. In all my long years I thought I truly understood what it meant to lead, but you humble me with your concern for my people, all my people, not just those who have a voice."

"Made sense to me," she whispered.

Gavriel rose and turned to those around him. "I feel I must share that it was also Meryn who suggested that Warrick reclaim his mother's name, establishing Fortier as a Founding Family as it should have been so long ago. She did so because it, 'made sense'." He paused dramatically. Serenity felt everyone's heart rates pick up. She looked around and saw awe and excitement on their faces. Gavriel placed his hand over his heart. "Maybe this suggestion of hers is also correcting a long term wrong we did not know even existed."

Hugo rubbed his chin. "What she says does make a lot of sense. Even with constant interaction it is nearly impossible to connect with all our citizens." His face became stony. "If what Prince Gavriel says is true, then we have failed to catch major transgressions. I am all for giving the citizens themselves a ruling seat in the form of a citizen led council."

Once the words were spoken everyone quickly agreed to Meryn's idea. Gavriel hopped back up on the stage to get everyone's attention. "We have seen and heard of terrible things, but, I think we also saw what hope looks like." He pointed to Warrick and Meryn. "Change is not always a bad thing. I, for one, am excited about our future," he said magnanimously. "That being said, please continue to support our efforts in healing the children. Thank you for coming, good day."

Once dismissed the crowd stood and began speaking to one another. There was a certain light in everyone's eyes as they threw out ideas on how to help organize this new Citizen Council.

Serenity was about to stand when she heard Meryn laughing. She looked around and saw that Kari was glaring at the small human.

Meryn stood and stretched. "She's gonna kill me." Serenity rose to her feet and looked down. "Did you plan that?"

Meryn shook her head. "Not really. I was talking

with Mr. Culpepper as I ate my meat kebobs and it kinda hit me that I was getting to attend these meetings and I don't even live here, but the people who work really hard to keep this place running don't get to come."

"You're kinda amazing, you know that right?"

Meryn shrugged. "I just see things differently."

"It's still amazing."

Meryn was about to respond when her eyes narrowed. "Oh, hell nah."

On Serenity's other side Micah's entire body tensed. When Meryn made a beeline for the stage, both Serenity and Micah were right behind her. While they had been talking, Prince Magnus and Beth had come into the meeting room and were speaking to people in front of the stage.

As Hugo walked away from Beth another man was approaching. As he was about to reach Beth, Meryn wedged her tiny body between them.

He looked down. "Excuse you," he sneered.

Meryn didn't back down. "No."

"What?" he demanded.

"Just because you say it, doesn't mean I have to do it."

The offensive man stepped right into Meryn's chest.

"Jourdain, I suggest you walk away," Micah growled.

"Meryn, let's go," Beth said softly, looking pale. Serenity walked over and wrapped an arm around her. Across the room she saw both Aiden and Gavriel distracted by different conversations. She felt a wave of relief when she saw Ryuu closing the distance between them at a rapid rate.

Meryn crossed her arms. "Get out of my personal space."

Jourdain gave her a smirk. "Just because you say it does not mean I have to do it," he repeated back at her.

"Look, standing this close I am going to assume one of two things. Either you want to fight me or fuck me. Either way, my mate will kill you," she said smugly.

Jourdain took a step back in shock at her words. When he snarled and leaned his face close to hers Serenity heard a faint popping sound, then Jourdain's eyes fluttered before they closed, and he hit the floor. Around them everyone stepped away looking down at the new Founding Family head in shock.

"Oh, dear," Beth said looking down.

Magnus reached them about the same time Ryuu did. He looked down at the twitching body. "Is he dead?" the prince asked, a bit of glee in his eyes.

Meryn shook her head and held up what looked like an odd wand. "Nope, but I shocked the shit out of him. It's my sonic screwdriver. I would have kicked him in the balls, but Aiden said I'm not allowed to do that casually anymore."

"Pity," Magnus murmured. "Though replacing the Régis family head for a second time in a half an hour would look bad."

"Some of us would not mind," Hugo said under his breath.

Ryuu held out his hand and Meryn handed him her screwdriver. It glowed blue for a moment and he handed back to her. "I have upped the charge for you."

Meryn eyed Jourdain's prone figure. Beth chuck-led. "No, Meryn."

"What did that bastard do to my Beth?" Gavriel roared. Sending people scurrying for the exit.

Micah was poking Jourdain with his foot. "Not a thing this time Gavriel. Meryn protected her."

"She what?" Aiden demanded. Both he and Gavriel turned to their mates and started looking them over.

Beth batted at Gavriel's hands laughing. "I am perfectly fine. He never even got near me. Meryn and Keelan protected me."

Serenity's breath caught. "Keelan?" she asked.

Beth pointed down at the device in Meryn's hand. "He made that for her."

"Why can't I kill him?" Aiden growled.

"Because I am running out of Founding Family members to promote," Magnus growled back.

Behind them Hugo, Javier, and Simon were propping themselves up while laughing themselves silly. Leana and Marie glared down at Jourdain. "It is about time someone put him in his place. He has been terrorizing poor Bethy for decades," Marie said.

Kari covered her face with both hands. "I cannot. I just cannot." Adriel was rubbing her shoulders and trying not to laugh.

Serenity pulled Micah away from Jourdain when he kept lightly kicking him to see if he would respond. "You are without a doubt the biggest goofball I have ever met."

He spun her around and dipped her low. "You knew that."

Serenity turned her head. Kari was still having a

bit of a meltdown, Aiden and Magnus were arguing that Jervasius had three sons, Gavriel was still looking Beth over and the other Founding Family heads were cackling like hyenas.

She looked back up at her mate as he held her in his arms. "So why does it kinda scare me that you're the normal one?"

He kissed her nose. "At least we're never boring."

CHAPTER TEN

M ICAH LOOKED DOWN AT HIS sleeping mate and quietly rapped on the arm of
the platform bed. He hoped the swaying motion
would keep her asleep until dinner. She had used
a lot of magic today and needed time to recharge.

He eased the door shut behind him and looked
over to where Hawthorne had made himself at
home in his living room. His feet were propped up
on the coffee table and he was on his iPad.

"Thanks again for watching after her."

Hawthorne grinned. "It's the easiest assignment
I've had all week. Does she know where you'll be?"

"Yes, I told her I'd be on Level One in a meeting
with Kendrick. I don't imagine her waking any
time soon though."

"I felt what she did at the hospital, she deserves
a break."

"She did even more during that Founding Family meeting." Micah glanced back at the door
leading to the garden. "Maybe I should stay here."

"You said that you needed to talk to Kendrick
while the kids were knocked out before it got

crazy again," Hawthorne reminded him.

"Shit. You're right."

"Go, on. I can manage here while you're gone."

"Okay, okay, I'm going. Thanks again."

"Anytime," Hawthorne said.

Micah left the house and jogged to the transport tunnel. He jumped down to Level One and headed straight to the Royal Garden. When he asked Kendrick if they could speak alone, Kendrick arranged for them to meet here to avoid being interrupted.

Kendrick was waiting for him by the door. "Right on time," he said and placed his hand on the door.

"You have access?" Micah asked.

"I pretty much have access everywhere except the vaults." He motioned with his hand. "After you."

Micah entered the garden and smiled. He always loved plants, a byproduct of being raised by an earth witch. They walked over and sat at the picnic benches the twins installed.

Kendrick folded his hands in front of him. "So, what did you want to see me about?"

Micah closed his eyes and cast the strongest soundproofing spell he could. Kendrick's eyes widened. "Micah is everything okay?" he looked around as if assessing any potential danger.

Micah took a deep breath. "After mating with Serenity, I told her some things about my family. She pretty much begged me to come to you for your help."

Kendrick's eyebrows snapped together as he frowned his concern. "I know I tease Serenity terribly, but there isn't much I wouldn't do for her.

She's the bratty kid sister I never had."

Micah hesitated. The next question would determine a lot. "What do you know about the massacre that happened five thousand years ago?"

Kendrick blinked. "What do you need to know?"

Micah stared. "You know of it?"

Kendrick slowly nodded. "Yes, but how do you?"

Micah shook his head. "Please, it's important. How do you know?"

Kendrick watched him for a moment before he answered. "My father told me about it. I was out of the country at the time."

"And how did he know?"

"He was there that night."

Micah exhaled. "So few remember the actual events of that night. I was fully expecting to have to peel back centuries of false memories before I could ask for your help." He wanted to lay his head on the table. "You have no idea how relieved I am that you're one of the very few who know."

"Micah, how do you know? You're not that old and you were raised in Storm Keep," Kendrick asked.

"You know about the mental manipulation."

Kendrick nodded. "But not exactly how it works."

"The most accurate theory I've read is that whatever magic was used that night permeated the stone of the Stormhart castle turning it into a broadcast tower constantly sending out the false narrative."

Kendrick leaned forward looking excited. "I never even thought about the castle itself, I thought it might be a powerful stone housed in one of the towers."

Micah shook his head. "One eye witness account reported that, for just a moment, the entire castle seemed to glow a faint red color, as if stained by the blood spilt that night."

"I have a copy of just about every book written about magic and the history of Storm Keep, I have never read any theories about the massacre or eye witness accounts." He eyed Micah closely. "Where are you getting your information."

Micah met his eyes, he didn't know if it was Serenity's influence, but he trusted Kendrick. "I am the bearer of the Veritas Book. It is a compilation of testimonies from different witches before their memories faded. We even have some accounts where the witch agreed to a type of regression therapy. They remembered long enough to tell us what they knew then they'd forget again."

Kendrick's hands started to visibly shake. "I need to read that book."

Micah shook his head. "I'm the only one allowed to read its pages. I have to read the entire thing at least once every other day or so, or even I start to forget some of the stories."

"Micah, you don't understand..." Kendrick started.

"I'm sorry Kendrick but my answer is no. Ever since that night five thousand years ago my family has worked and died creating this book. I'm not trying to be difficult, but my family swore an oath to our true king and queen and I won't be the one to break it. My duty is to not only reveal to the world what happened but to also make the ones responsible pay for what they've done."

Kendrick blinked back tears. Micah felt terrible. "I know it's overwhelming to hear at first..."

Kendrick stood and walked around the table. Micah thought for sure he was going to take a swing and was shocked when he was pulled to his feet and into a massive hug.

"Uh, Kendrick. We're both mated..."

Kendrick began to chuckle. When he stepped back Micah could see tears on his cheeks. "Okay. Great meeting, I gotta go."

"My name is Julian Stormhart. My parents were driven from Storm Keep five thousand years ago and the only ones who could have possibly accomplished all you've said are the supposedly murdered members of the Whiteoak family. The intelligence agency my mother created," Kendrick drew in a shaky breath.

Micah's chest constricted and his throat closed. For some reason he couldn't seem to get any air. He grabbed at his throat and looked up at Kendrick in a panic.

Kendrick's hand went to his back forcing him to bend in half. "Easy, shallow breaths. In. Out. In. Out," he said softly.

"D-d-dyin-n-g," Micah gasped. He turned to look up at the man allowing him to die.

"No, you're not dying, you're having a panic attack," Kendrick said grinning down at him.

Kendrick eased him back onto the bench and sat down next to him facing the opposite direction as he leaned against the table. "Better?"

Micah kept a hand on his chest. "I think so." He glared at him. "Why aren't you dead?"

Kendrick raised a brow. "How do you exist? My

mother was certain that her closest friends died giving them time to escape. She said it was as if the castle rose up to fight off the attackers, but it wasn't enough."

Micah blinked repeatedly. Kendrick said mother, but he was talking about their queen, his queen! Kendrick nudged him. "Right. Sorry. My gran was training with a unit and survived. She's the one who started the book.

"My family started serving yours before the end of the Great War. Your mother used the intelligence they gathered to avoid bloody battles. After the war ended, they followed the royal couple and took up different positions in the castle.

"The Ashleighs became the sword and the Iron-woods the shield. They were meant to be seen, respected and feared to do their jobs. But my family had to blend in to do their jobs, so they became the maids, the cooks, the stable hands and every other possible position that would give them the most access to the kingdom.

"The Ashleighs and the Ironwoods lost the elder generation the ones who lived in the castle, but the younger ones survived because they lived together on larger estates next to the castle.

"Your mother was right. One entry in the book said, that on the night of the attack, the intruders were engaged at every turn. Nearly every servant, *my* family, took up arms and it was barely enough to get them out alive."

Kendrick shook his head. "That book. The missing piece of the puzzle. The only thing in existence that could prove to others that something did happen five thousand years ago."

Micah spun on the bench to face him. "Why haven't you done anything? You could have taken back the city..." He stopped Kendrick just smirked at him. "Right, it's hard to take a back a city when they don't remember who you are."

Kendrick gave a one shoulder shrug. "And I was protecting something very important." Micah frowned. Kendrick continued. "My brother Keelan."

Micah felt his chest constrict. Kendrick whacked him a few times. "We're not doing this again."

"Keelan is hurt!" Micah shouted. Keelan was one of his princes. The last of the line he was sworn to protect.

"Yes, I know. Though, technically he isn't hurt at all, he's just not in his body at the moment."

"Can't you put him back in?" Micah asked.

Kendrick nodded then shook his head. "He's busy at the moment acting as the intelligence portion of the perimeter protecting Lycaonia."

"The purple fireworks," Micah whispered.

Kendrick chuckled. "In the centuries that Keelan served as a unit warrior I had no idea the craziness and fun he experienced in his day to day life. Do you know that Aiden thinks little human girls are ninjas?"

"Why?" Micah asked feeling thoroughly confused.

"He listened to Colton," Kendrick explained.

"You do realize those two are the highest-ranking unit warriors in the country, don't you," Micah pointed out.

Kendrick smiled. "Amazing isn't it?" His smiled faded a bit. "You should see those two fight. Never in all my years have I ever seen anything that comes close to how beautiful they look when fighting in hand-to-hand combat, standing back to back with each other."

"Beautiful?" Micah asked skeptically.

Kendrick just nodded. "I think it's because they were raised side by side. Even before they received any training, they were toddling around together in diapers. It's almost like Colton is an extension of Aiden when they're fighting. They just know instinctively where the other is." He looked Micah in the eye. "Without magic, there's no way I could take them and I've studied different fighting techniques for thousands of years."

"I really want to see them fight now," Micah confessed.

Kendrick stared into the distance. "They're also the best because they never leave a man behind. The day Elder Airgead tried to kill us, the council building was coming down, I had given up, but the Alpha Unit was waiting for me in the hallway." He shook his head. "I owe them much."

Micah's mouth dropped. "What in the hell do you mean when Elder Airgead tried to kill you?"

Kendrick winced. "Oh yeah, you only heard the edited version." He took a deep breath and began retelling him the actual events of that day and the ramifications of what it all meant.

Micah swallowed hard. "Your parents..."

Kendrick's jaw clenched. "Still trapped."

"I swear to you on my life, I will not rest until they are free," Micah vowed.

Kendrick just stared at him. "Thank you. I've long since forgotten what it felt like to have the loyalty of such a dedicated family." He tilted his head, reminding Micah of Meryn. "Why didn't you go to the Ashleighs or the Ironwoods?"

Micah just stared. "They know?"

Kendrick held up his finger. "So far, only Marshall Ironwood and Lily Camden know. The truth kinda came out at dinner when they were visiting Amelia. In fact, the entire Alpha Unit knows." He rubbed the back of his neck. "I haven't told the Ashleighs yet."

Micah barked out his laughter. "Thane is going to kill you," he predicted.

Kendrick winced. "Yes, I'm not really looking forward to that conversation, though I know it's coming soon. I pulled Marshall off his mission to find my parents. The Ashleighs listened to Marshall when he reported in because they respect him, but I know they sent multiple agents to check to make sure Marshall and Lily aren't under any influence or being coerced."

"Have they met Lily Camden?" he joked. That woman was a force of nature.

Kendrick gave him an evil smile. "You mean Meryn's biological aunt?"

"Who in the hell is this little human?" Micah asked. It seemed like every time they turned around Meryn was at the center of things.

"Believe me, I know exactly what you mean. She is under my protection at the moment, if only because Anne simply adores her."

"And she adopted your cousins," Micah said slyly. He took great satisfaction at the way the blood drained from Kendrick's face. He owed him after his identity reveal.

Kendrick was now the one standing with a hand on his chest. "What! No! That's impossible. They-they-they..."

"Breathe. In. Out. In. Out," Micah teased.

Kendrick took a moment to collect himself. "It's not true."

Micah nodded. "Actually, it is. Remember, my family deals in truth and secrets. Your father's cousin was murdered that night, but his mistress lived. She gave birth and the child lived happily in ignorance and ambiguity. My gran kept tabs on that line thinking they were the last of the Stormharts. The twins' parents were assigned out and never returned to Storm Keep so the boys were placed in the orphanage. There were a few times when she almost yanked them out, but decided it was safer not to bring attention to them." Micah pointed up at Kendrick. "You helped raise your cousins and didn't even know it."

Kendrick sat back down abruptly returning to his place on the bench. "It's been just me and Kee for so long, then Kee..." His eyes narrowed. "Is that twisted son of bitch still in charge at the orphanage?"

Micah nodded. "Why you gonna kill him?" he asked flippantly. When Kendrick turned to face him, his eyes held such murderous rage that it shocked him. Micah shook his head. "Poor bastard doesn't even know he's already dead."

Kendrick growled. "Like your gran, I didn't interfere because I didn't want to make things worse for them and legally I had no recourse, but now that I know..." he trailed off.

Micah saw Kendrick grinding his teeth. He

reached over and patted his leg. "Look on the bright side. At least that red hair stayed in the family."

Kendrick gave a sad smile. "It was the reason why I left, the court nobles said I didn't look like my father. They didn't really know about recessive genes back then." He chuckled. "After my parents were driven away from Storm Keep my father loved tending his garden. Over the years, that much time in the sun turned his hair auburn. I finally saw where I got my hair."

Micah rotated on the bench so he could lean against the table as well. "What do we do now?"

"Eventually I would like to read your Veritas Book." He rubbed his jaw. "For now, we concentrate on curing this virus. Once we're able to leave the city I think a sit-down meeting with the Ironwoods and the Ashleighs is long overdue." He turned his head. "Our enemy is still out there. That level of mass mental manipulation..." He looked around. "Gods! That's why you're here isn't it?"

"Taking my warrior exam was one of the hardest things I had to do. I had to score high enough to be placed with Eta, but low enough that they wouldn't keep me in the city."

"Have you found anything?" Kendrick asked.

"Loads, but nothing concrete enough to explain what happened five thousand years ago. Unfortunately, I've found that vampire abilities are very subjective.

"For example. One day a vendor on Level Six could hear the thoughts of those around her. She described it like her mind had tuned into one station for the day. The following day the ability was gone. In another case a woman was assaulted by her own mate. Unbeknownst to him his anger at her lashed out in her mind. He was absolutely guilt-stricken but swore up and down he had no idea he was doing it.

"The older vampires have more control, but even then, they have to concentrate solely on a single person. Unless we're talking about a vampire with extraordinary abilities, then you would need at least a couple thousand vampires to pull off what happened in Storm Keep."

"Did you only talk to women?" Kendrick asked curiously.

Micah nodded. "Women were easier to get close to. Sadly, most of them simply wanted someone to listen to them." He looked down at his hands. "I've been lying to my unit brothers all these years. My true purpose in getting assigned to Noctem Falls was to learn as much as I could about vampire abilities. I feel like I've betrayed their trust."

"That's not necessarily true. You never outright lied to them and according to Adriel you're the best unit witch in the city. I believe you have gone above and beyond in carrying out your unit warrior duties. You just had things you couldn't tell them. You weren't being deceitful, you were keeping them and many others safe. A single mission can carry two purposes Micah," Kendrick said in a firm, but kind voice.

In that moment Micah knew he was in the presence of his king. "What would you have me do?" he asked. Kendrick could ask him to do pretty much anything that wouldn't put Serenity in danger and he would do it. By asking that question he wanted Kendrick to know that he had his undying loyalty.

Kendrick looked startled at what the question implied, then composed himself. "Flirt. Enjoy being mated. Protect your warrior brothers and the city you serve. There will come a time when I will need your help, but until then, live each day to the fullest. We have dark days ahead and we will need these days to carry us through."

"I can definitely flirt," Micah admitted trying to lighten the atmosphere.

"Don't let your mate hear that. She can literally tie your nuts in knots. I taught her the spell myself."

"Can I tell her about you?"

Kendrick grimaced. "She may end up tying my nuts in knots. But go ahead anyway. There shouldn't be secrets between mates." He looked over at him. "What about the Alpha Unit? Technically they don't have to know that you exist, but since they know everything else it might work in our advantage to have their help later."

"Meryn knows about you?" Micah asked.

Kendrick smiled smugly. "She figured it out on her own based on the last name I chose to return to the city with."

"Ashwood. How did I miss that?" Micah felt like it was obvious now that he knew. "If we tell Alpha about me, can we tell Eta about you?"

Kendrick was silent for a few minutes. "If the men turned out to be anyone but who they are I'd say no. But Adriel is related to Gavriel. Declan is a member of the most political savvy shifter Founding Family in the world, Grant's brother leads the largest wolf pack in the country and he's an Alpha

Born, and Etain's family have always served Queen Aleksandra who already knows who I am." He clapped him on the back. "Then there's you. One of the last surviving members of the family my parents trusted the most. I believe I will let you use your judgement on whether to tell Eta and the others or not."

Micah groaned as Kendrick placed that decision in his lap. He started going over everyone else holding up fingers as he went. "It's a given that if the men know, their mates will know as well. Which considering those special ladies I don't think it will be a problem. Magnus of course is a given, along with Caspian since he is a royal, so Broderick will be told. Rex for the same reasons as Declan, probably even more so. Marjoram won't care one way or another she'll still fuss at you and make you cookies." He frowned. "We may have to shackle Law beforehand though, so he doesn't strangle you." He put down his hands having run out of fingers. "Avery, Warrick, Pip and the twins haven't been eating with us at night very much. I'd trust Warrick with my life and I know Avery would never betray us. It just isn't in him. I trust the twins, but they are young. The only ones I'm unsure of are Laelia and Radclyffe Juniper, Pip and whichever guard will be in the room at the time."

Kendrick turned to him. "Laelia and Radclyffe will be fine. They are dedicated heart and soul to the people of Storm Keep. They may actually be needed to act as points of contact in the city, along with your gran of course." Kendrick ran a hand over his mouth. "The twins would rather eat glass than do or say anything to hurt me. They are young, but everyone always underestimates what they've lived through."

"What about Pip?"

"I am going to trust Fate. She brought Pip into our circle for a reason and according to Meryn, he's family now. You didn't mention the squires," Kendrick pointed out.

Micah rolled his eyes. "I've never met better squires in all my life. They would break a confidence right after they killed their charges."

Micah stood and took down the sound proof spell. "Well, dinner will be fun."

Kendrick rose and chewed on his lower lip. "So, shackles for Law, right?" Micah laughed. Kendrick continued. "And you must keep your mate from twisting my nuts, Anne is fond of them."

"You're the big, bad, witch. I'm sure you can handle them," Micah said as they walked out of the garden.

"Go ahead and joke, you've never seen your mate pissed. I have. She is terrifying," Kendrick shuddered.

"You're more scared of my sweet Serenity than you are of Law Ashleigh?" Micah asked.

"You have no idea," Kendrick warned.

In that moment Micah realized he had a new goal in life. To never, ever piss off his mate.

Micah looked down at his mate and wondered what she had done in the past to make Kendrick so afraid of her. All he could see were soft dark curls and creamy skin. Her mouth was moving slightly as if she was talking in her dreams. He loathed to awaken her, but in an effort to avoid her getting mad at him he decided to wake her, so she'd have time to get ready.

"Serenity, my one and only, time to wake up," he said gently.

"No," she murmured and turned her face way from him.

"I made you a fresh pot of coffee," he said, enticingly.

"Fresh?" she asked, her head popping up.

"Yes. In fact, you have enough time to enjoy a cup before getting ready for dinner." He wanted brownie points for his efforts.

Her bright smile almost had him throwing his good intentions aside, she was so damn beautiful his body was making its own demands.

"I love you so much," she said in a breathy voice. She stretched and swung her legs over the side of the bed. "Where is that wonderful coffee?"

"On the counter. I left a cup out for you."

She pecked him on the cheek. "Coffee, coffee, coffee," she sang as she walked into the house.

Micah could only hope she'd keep her happy mood after tonight's revelations. Something told him it was going to take more than coffee to calm her down later. He shrugged. Like he told his mate earlier, at least they weren't bored.

CHAPTER ELEVEN

SERENITY KEPT TURNING TO LOOK at Micah as dinner started. His heart rate was high, and he was sweating. She was about to ask him what was wrong when Kendrick stood.

"Ryuu, can you ask Hal and Sebastian to step into the room please?" he asked. Ryuu gave a half bow and went through the swinging door to the kitchen, moments later the squires walked back through pushing their serving carts and stood to one side.

Kendrick took a deep breath then lifted his hands at either side of his body. The spell he released not only sound proofed the room, but sealed it as well. No one could accidentally walk in.

Magnus leaned back. "That important?"

Kendrick nodded. "What I am about to share can go no further." He looked around the table. "Where are Warrick, Avery, Pip and the twins?"

"Avery wanted to introduce Pip to my zombie game, so they convinced Marjoram to cook for them on the Unit Level. She's up there now probably giving away my cookies," Meryn said looking perturbed.

"You know gram would never do that Meryn," Ellie chided.

Kendrick turned to Sebastian. "Are we expecting Pavil?"

Sebastian shook his head. "Given the events of the day, I thought a light dinner would be best. It does not take four squires to serve soup and sandwiches. Pavil is taking the night off with Bree."

Kendrick looked to Tarak. "I will need your word that what is discussed will go no further, with the exception of your brother."

Tarak nodded. "You have my word."

Kendrick turned back to the table. "In fact, I will need everyone's word that what is said here will remain amongst us. It's not that I don't trust you, I wouldn't be sharing what I know if I didn't, but I need you to know that lives could be lost if what is said gets out." Serenity nodded along with everyone else. Under the table Micah took her hand. She glanced up at him, his normally laughing eyes were somber. She squeezed his hand gently and he gave a nod.

Kendrick began telling the story of what happened five thousand years ago in Storm Keep, how the king and queen were driven out of their home and how the entire country was made to forget. Varying expressions of disbelief were clearly visible around the table. Only those visiting from Lycaonia didn't look shocked.

Adriel stared up at Kendrick. "You would not be sharing this for no reason. What changed that prompted you to divulge this information?"

Kendrick's eyes flicked to Micah. Serenity was

shocked when he rose to his feet beside her.

"Because I told him who I am and why I'm here," Micah started.

Adriel's face became unreadable. "Go on."

"What Kendrick said is true. Five thousand years ago the witch council rose to power almost over-night and no one questioned it. I know, because my family was amongst those murdered that night. Only my gran survived. Since then she and others have been gathering evidence trying to ascertain how so many people could be manipulated at once."

"So you came to the city of the vampires to investigate our powers?" Magnus asked quietly.

Micah simply nodded. "I did everything I could to be assigned here. It was my mission to learn all there was to know about the vampire's abilities to control the mind."

Adriel's jaw clenched. "Was any of what you said and did over the centuries real? Or were you just using us to learn what you could?" he asked coldly.

Etain faced his unit leader. "Do not let your emotions say what you do not mean. Micah gave of himself many times over since being assigned to Eta. He guarded your mate, kept Declan alive after he was attacked and saved my daughter. He may have been trying to investigate the vampires, but he was a unit warrior as he was doing it."

Beside her Micah's eyes were bright. "Thank you, Etain."

Rex looked around. "I don't see what the prob-lem is. We all have things we cannot share because of split loyalties. I am first and foremost a Lionhart, I protect my family and the shifters that look to us.

My second loyalty is to Queen Aleksandra, as she opened up Eiré Danu to the lions. My personal position as Elder comes third. But that doesn't mean I don't care for the people of Noctem Falls."

Magnus nodded. "Well said." He turned to Adriel. "I know you are feeling hurt, but remember, that you are feeling hurt because you care so much for this young man."

"Of course I do!" Adriel exploded in a rare display of emotion. "He is not only a fellow warrior, but my unit brother. What I am most angry about is that he did not come to us for help." He crossed his arms over his chest and sat back.

Eva's mouth twitched. "Are you pouting? Because if you are, it's adorable."

"I am not pouting!" Adriel argued, not realizing he made the perfect picture of a petulant child.

Declan turned to him. "You said your family was murdered, why them?"

Micah smiled looking proud. "My family is descended from the druidic line of Darwid, meaning oak and to know. The more commonly used name is Whiteoak."

Gavriel sat up and leaned forward. "*The* Whiteoaks. The family that dedicated its entire line to intelligence gathering?" he asked looking excited. Micah nodded. Gavriel shook his head. "What in the hell are we facing that so many threads are being woven together?"

"There's more," Kendrick said rubbing the back of his neck.

Magnus chuckled. "What more could you possibly say? Tonight has given us back a prestigious family that we thought was lost."

Kendrick chuckled. "Yeah, about that."

Micah threaded his hands behind his head. "Go on," he urged.

Kendrick's eyes flicked to Serenity then back to Micah. Micah laughed. "Stop being a big baby, she won't kill you."

Serenity scowled up at Kendrick. "What is he talking about? Why would I kill you?"

Kendrick straightened, and Serenity saw a visible change come over him. He no longer slouched, and his power crackled around him. "The reason we shared with you Micah's true purpose and name, is because I will be calling him to service in the not to distant future and he will need to be released from his unit duties."

Adriel bristled, and he looked from Aiden to Kendrick and back. "Aiden is our Unit Commander, only he can change our orders. What are you planning on doing with Micah," he demanded.

"Aww you do care," Micah teased.

Serenity swatted him. "Micah hush."

"Yes, my one and only," he responded looking pleased.

Aiden turned to Adriel. "When the time comes I will be releasing not only Micah, but also Caiden, Kyran and Tristan Ironwood." He looked to Law. "I have a feeling you and your brothers will be pressed into service as well."

Law snorted. "There isn't a single person alive, save our mother, who can tell me and my brothers what to do."

Micah brought his hands down and wiggled them at Law. "Air shackles whenever you're ready Kendrick," he said playfully.

Kendrick turned to Adriel. "You may end up keeping that one," he said jerking his thumb to Micah.

Serenity's mind raced. Why would Aiden release Micah and the Ironwoods to serve Kendrick? How did the Ashleighs fit into all this? Ashleigh, Ironwood, and Whiteoak? She inhaled sharply choking on her own spit. She began to choke with sent her into a spiral of panic. There was no way.

Kendrick looked at her pleased then turned to Law. "She's smarter than you."

Law scowled up at Kendrick. "What in the hell are you talking about?"

Micah sat back down and rubbed her back. "There, there darling. You're having the same reaction I did earlier this afternoon." He pressed her water goblet to her lips. "Take a sip."

"Micah, is she okay?" Laelia asked worriedly.

"She'll be just fine," Micah replied.

To Serenity, the ice-cold water felt good going down. She focused on slowing her breathing. If she didn't get herself under control Laelia and Radclyffe would start mollycoddling her. When she looked up it was like she was seeing Kendrick for the first time. "How?" she whispered.

"Oh, my gods," Kari said, slumping back on her chair.

Kendrick held up two fingers. "That's two ladies who beat you to it Law."

Law looked around and besides herself, Kari and those from Lycaonia, everyone else wore a confused expression. He turned to Kendrick. "What has Serenity choking and my baby sister Kari looking like she's about to faint? Why would Micah threaten me with air shackles," he demanded furiously.

"Probably because of your temper," Serenity answered taking a deep breath. She stood on shaky legs and Micah rose with her. They both turned to face Kendrick and she dropped to a deep curtsy while Micah bowed.

Law popped Micah on the arm. "Stop that. What in the world is going on? Why would you bow to Kendrick?"

His question sent Meryn into a fit of giggles. "Maybe we should have Sebastian scrounge up a two-by-four, so you can beat him over the head with the answer."

"Now, Meryn. It isn't very obvious," Aiden chided.

Meryn sniffed. "I was the first person to figure it out back home."

"Micah Whiteoak, Serenity Meadowsweet, please rise," Kendrick said formally.

All her life Serenity hated the way Storm Keep was ruled. Everyone was so obsessed with their test scores that the brighter days of their king and queen had fallen to legend and myth. In her heart, she always felt that, as a people, they should be doing more.

She couldn't believe the humble archivist who lived in the Lower City for centuries was their long, lost king.

As the truth hit her sobs broke free and her tears ran unchecked down her face. Micah wrapped an arm around her, no less affected. He stared at Kendrick with a look of absolute devotion tears dripping off his chin.

Kari wiped at her eyes. "That is just beautiful."

Law stood angrily and faced Kendrick. "You and me outside. I am tired of questions answering questions."

Kari laughed. "Law, do not threaten to beat your king, as an Ashleigh you are sworn to protect him." Her words rang around the table, everyone stared at Kendrick who raised an eyebrow to Law.

"Well?"

The blood drained from Law's face so quickly Serenity was sure he was going to keel over. "That's...just...not...possible," he managed to croak out, grabbing at his chair to stay upright.

Kendrick straightened his back and turned to face the table. "My name is Julian Stormhart, son of Kiran and Celeste Stormhart. I hope you will be able to keep my secret and when the time comes, help me and my people."

Laelia and Radclyffe jumped to their feet bowing. "Your Majesty," they said.

"Laelia, Radclyffe rise. Treat me as you always have, after the sound proof spell is taken down, I'll be just Kendrick again." When they stood straight and stared at him Kendrick raised a brow to Radclyffe. "Still want to make bondage jokes?"

Radclyffe gave a strangled groan and bowed again. "I am so sorry."

Laelia pulled him back up laughing. "Your Majesty, that was just mean," she admonished. Kendrick just chuckled.

Anne rolled her eyes. "Ignore him. He thinks he's so witty when his ego swells." She popped Kendrick on the ass. "I'll deflate him later."

Kendrick leered down at her. "I know something

you can deflate."

Magnus gripped the table with both hands. "Help you with what exactly?" he asked.

Kendrick gave them the sarcastic smile they were all used to. "Help me take back my city and free my people."

His words ignited the table into a flurry of questions. Serenity continued to stare, heedless of the chaos around her. Kendrick looked over and winked. He may be her king, but he was her friend first.

"I'm tired of standing and I'm starving. If you're done being magnificent can Sebastian, Hal and Ryuu serve us dinner?" she asked sitting back down.

Micah cracked his back. "I think all that bowing pulled a muscle." He sat down next to her.

Laelia and Radclyffe were staring at her as if she lost her mind. But she knew she did the right thing when Kendrick gave her a look of gratitude.

"Yeah, I'm hungry," Meryn chimed in.

Kendrick sat back down and placed his napkin in his lap. "What kind of sandwiches do we have tonight?"

Laelia and Radclyffe sat down slowly as if unsure they should and Law was still standing, blinking at Kendrick.

Kendrick pointed to Law's chair. "Sit," he said.

It was as if the strings holding up Law were cut. He collapsed down in his chair.

"Roll over," Meryn teased.

Law turned to Meryn scowling. "Ease up tater tot, it's not every day one learns that their king has returned."

"Return of the King, that was a great movie," Meryn said nodding.

Hal still looked distracted as he began to walk around the table with his tray of sandwiches. Ryuu and Sebastian, however, looked unruffled as they began to serve.

Ryuu started with Meryn. "*Denka*, I made sure to make Colton's famous sandwich as it is a favorite of yours."

"Can I get two?" she asked. He nodded and placed two sandwiches on her plate.

Aiden held up his plate. "Five for me please."

Declan exchanged looks with Grant. "What's a Colton sandwich," he asked.

Grant shrugged. "I'm not sure, but since it's named for Colton, I'm staying away from them."

Declan nodded. "Good point."

"Hey! I'll have you know that my sandwich is amazing. It's a culinary masterpiece consisting of mayo, peanut butter, cheese, pickles and beef jerky."

Grant cringed. "Definitely staying away."

Adriel turned to Magnus his left eye twitching. "Are we supposed to ignore the statement he made about retaking his city?"

Magnus sighed. "Yes. There is not much we can do about it at the moment anyway. Our own city is still being ravaged by that damn virus."

Ellie turned to Vivi as the squires continued to serve. "Did you make any progress toward a cure?"

Vivi sniffled loudly, tears in her eyes. "Backwards engineering a cure takes time."

"We are out of time," Ellie whispered.

Colton leaned forward so he could see Vivi. "Why can't we just use older vampire blood like we planned. We know the problem with Magnus was due to the transition elements in Gavriel's blood."

Vivi shook her head. "I hadn't factored any transition markers into the cure. I normally work with younger vampire blood, so this issue never came up before. But the older the vampire, the more markers their blood carries, the more aggression is triggered. It was a blessing in disguise that Magnus had an adverse reaction. As a vampire the markers simply triggered a transition in his body. But shifters don't go through transition, they don't have a way to process the markers. They would stay feral."

Ellie turned to Serenity. "How much time do they have?"

Serenity shook her head. "Tomorrow evening at the very latest. Their little bodies are worn out. They don't have any fight left in them."

Ellie covered her face with both hands and wept. Grant pulled her close to his body and kissed the top of her head. Around the table her words triggered many to tears.

Serenity wrung her hands. "I wish we could do more."

Micah placed his hand over hers. "This fight started long before you got here. Don't take this on yourself."

Laelia and Radclyffe stood. "Kendrick if you could remove the barrier, we'd like to make sure the children are as comfortable as possible. We'd also like to start strengthening the parents."

Kendrick closed his eyes and the air flexed. They were still covered by the soundproof spell, but the barrier was gone. "Don't hesitate to call if you need anything."

Sebastian laid a hand on Laelia's shoulder. "I'll send up sandwiches, soup and coffee in a bit."

"Thank you," Radclyffe said looking relieved. Serenity could tell he was worried about his mate. They waved goodbye and headed out.

Eva looked up at her mate. "We need to meet with Stefan, the parents will need the support of the pack."

Magnus slammed his hands on the table as he stood. Without saying a word, he walked out of the dining room. Beth buried her face in Gavriel's shoulder.

Caspian took a deep breath. "This will scar him. I know my brother. For him to live as the children die, it will change him."

"I'm doing all I can!" Vivi cried. Etain scooted back and lifted her up into his lap.

Hal hurried to their side to run a hand over her hair. "You have to calm down baby girl, for your daughter's sake."

When Ellie went to stand Grant pulled her back down. "No. You need to eat and get some rest. Especially if tomorrow..." he couldn't finish the sentence.

"We've come all this way, come so far. It can't end like this," Rheia said bitterly.

Serenity watched as Gavriel and Kendrick exchanged a sad look. It shook her when she realized what that look meant. Both were thousands of years old, how many good people had they watch die needlessly? It was a look of commiseration, as they mentally added the children to a running tally of grief they bore witness to.

Magnus walked back into the room and sat down looking calmer. He turned to look at her. "Is there nothing you can do?" he asked.

Serenity shook her head. "I am so sorry. But there's no magic in the world that can simply cure a disease or sickness. Our bodies are constantly creating cells and metabolizing energy. The processes are extremely intricate. My magic acts as a tool, I use it the same way a doctor would use medicine or surgery. I focus on altering a certain chemical to get the reaction I need like putting someone to sleep, easing their anxiety or reducing a fever. I can encourage bone growth or keep a wound open, but if I were to pour my magic into trying to cure a virus its ever-changing nature would deplete me of my life-force." She looked around the room and wanted to ease everyone's pain and worry. These people had been through enough.

Magnus rubbed both hands over his face. "Forgive me, I knew the answer but asked anyway. They are just babies. They have barely experienced anything this world has to offer. If I could take my remaining years and spread it amongst them I would, in a heartbeat." His head hung low. "I feel like this is all my fault. Those children should have been safe here."

Kari lay a hand on his shoulder. "Place the blame where it belongs, with DeLaFontaine and the evil men he was conspiring with."

Magnus lifted his face and the grief there was soul shattering. "There are so few children being born, for us to lose so many, all at once, is a tragedy we may not recover from."

Serenity thought of Laelia and Radclyffe and

their desperate attempts to have a child. She couldn't imagine finally conceiving, giving birth raising them for years only to lose them. She knew that some parents in that hospital had more than one child ill, what would happen to them if they lost all their children? There had to be something she could do.

Meryn tapped at the table absently. "I feel like I'm missing something."

Anne wiped at her eyes. "Then we probably have, you're usually right when it comes to these things."

Meryn looked over at Rheia. "It was something you said that started a niggle in my brain."

Rheia gave a sad smile. "A niggle huh?"

Vivi turned to Meryn. "If you think of anything, no matter how small please let me know. I won't make the mistake of underestimating you again."

"Thanks." Meryn said then her eyes narrowed. "Wait a minute, you underestimated me?" She crossed her arms over her chest. "Heifer."

Vivi blew her nose in the hanky Hal provided. "I simply adore you too Gizmo."

Meryn was about to respond when Stefan's frantic voice came through Eva's walkie-talkie. "Eva! Please come quick and bring the doctors. The kids are crashing!"

Everyone stared at each other for a moment in horror before they stood and catapulted into action. Serenity and Micah were right behind Ellie and Rheia as they ran for the tunnel. The distance between Level One and the hospital never seemed so long before.

When they ran into the hospital parents were wailing and holding still bodies in their arms. The

hospital machines beeped and shrilled out warn-
ings and alerts. But all Serenity saw were her two
best friends in standing in the middle of the room.
Back to back they held out their hands sending
threads of magic to each child.

"No!" she screamed, when she realized what
they were doing. They were trying to use their
own lives to anchor the children and buy them
time, but at a dreadful cost. A cost she would not
allow them to pay.

"Serenity, what's going on?" Micah asked, spinning her around to face him.

She knew what she had to do, but her heart
protested leaving her mate. She reached up and
cupped his cheek and time seemed to stand still.

"I am grateful for those stolen moments Fate
gave us the night of our claiming. She gave us an
entire lifetime in one night, and you know what, it
was worth it," she whispered. "I hope you can find
it in your heart to forgive me."

She used her magic to send a pulse into him daz-
ing him for a moment. Her magic had always been
stronger than her friends. She placed her hand on
their shoulders and shoved them apart sending
them flying to the floor. She took their place at the
apex they created and lovingly began to gather the
threads to the core of her magic.

She knew nothing about science or labs or markers, but she did know magic. She knew the body's
inborn sense to fight and live. She called on that
instinct now as she sent her own power down the
threads to the tiny bodies struggling to cling to life.

*You will live. You will live and grow and laugh and
love. And someday if you're very lucky Fate will give you*

mate as wonderful as mine. It isn't time for you to go.

Slowly the world around her faded as she concentrated on holding on to those precious threads.

Micah blinked, then blinked again. When his eyes focused he turned to see Laelia and Radclyffe staring up at Serenity. Laelia had her fist in her mouth as she sobbed and Radclyffe clutched at his chest.

The last thing he remembered was the look of sorrow on his mate's face. The way she begged for his forgiveness. Micah felt like someone had punched him in the stomach.

"Adriel!" he yelled, calling out for the one brother who always knew what to do.

"I am here," Adriel said, wrapping an arm around his upper chest.

"I have to stop her! Help me!" he begged, he struggled to step forward, but another set of hands held him back.

"Kendrick said she is too far into the spell, if we pull her out we'll lose them all," Declan explained quickly, supporting him from his other side.

"None of your nightmares came true! It's not fair!" he pushed at their hands. "Give her back!" he pleaded.

Where there once were wails and crying, the room was eerily silent as he struggled against his unit brothers. The parents wept for him, knowing that his mate somehow gave their children a chance. She sacrificed herself to give Vivi more time to find a cure for the children.

Kendrick stepped into his field of vision blocking his view of his mate. "Forgive me," he whispered, echoing Serenity's last words to him.

"No!" he raged as Kendrick's hand touched his forehead and darkness claimed him.

CHAPTER TWELVE

WHEN MICAH OPENED HIS EYES, he felt like he was waking up in a fog. He looked around. Why was he in one of Magnus' guest rooms? Meryn anxiously watched him, her green eyes wide.

Reality ripped the fog away. "Serenity," he gasped.

Meryn rushed over and sat on the bed. "Hush! If you freak out again, Kendrick will zap you for your own good. You can't help her if you're unconscious." She placed both of her hands on his chest. "She's still alive Micah, we just have to figure out how to get her back."

He shook his head. "You don't understand. She tied the kids to the core of her magic. Every second that passes they drain more of her life away."

Meryn's eyes hardened. "As long as she's breathing, there is hope."

"What have I missed?" he asked, sitting up.

Meryn hopped off the bed and returned to her chair. "Everyone is losing their shit. Kendrick is pacing back and forth snarling at people. Vivi, Ellie and Rheia have locked themselves in the lab,

Etain, Colton and Grant are threatening to break the door down and Laelia and Radclyffe refuse to leave the hospital. They have been doing everything they can to help the kids to lessen Serenity's burden."

"Why are you in here with me?" he asked.

She shrugged. "Where else would I be? I'm not medically trained, and everyone is using the antechamber as base camp. It's quieter in here with you."

A throat cleared. "And she was worried about you," Ryuu added.

"Way to put me out there Ryuu," Meryn said blushing.

"Meryn, you're the one who keeps figuring things out." He stood and took her hand. "Come on my delicate flower, my one and only needs your genius."

He led Meryn to the antechamber, Ryuu behind them. When he walked in everyone quieted. The looks of remorse and sorrow on the faces of his unit brothers were almost his undoing.

"Okay people. How do we get her back?" he asked, steering Meryn into her recliner.

Declan pulled him into a hug. "We've been talking things out, trying to think of other ways we can help the kids."

Micah clapped Declan on the shoulder. "The only thing that will save my mate is a cure for the children. Once they are solidly anchored by their own life forces she will be able to break free from the spell."

"That's what I've been telling them," Kendrick said sourly.

Anne just looked up at her mate. "Actually, you been snapping at everyone and throwing your arms in the air."

Kendrick looked down at Anne. "I've known her since she was a child. It's like losing Keelan all over again," he whispered.

Anne jumped to her feet and wrapped her arms around his waist. "We haven't lost Keelan and we're not going to lose Serenity either," she said rubbing his back.

"Okay, someone break this down for me," Meryn said, crossing her legs.

Adriel looked at Meryn, though his eyes were kind, his expression was exasperated. "I do not think we have time to explain the science or the magic."

Meryn leaned over and dangled off the side of the recliner. She unclipped her walkie-talkie. "ViThreePO, come in."

"Meryn? Is everything okay?" Vivi's voice came back.

"The men think they know everything and won't explain things to me. Can you guys come to the antechamber?"

"We just started a test, once we have it running, we'll be right there," Vivi promised.

Magnus turned to Meryn with a pained expression. "Is it necessary to pull them from the lab?"

Meryn simply crossed her arms over her chest and ignored him. Magnus winced. "Meryn you know I trust you but..."

"But I'm not a scientist? Guess what? I'm not a military leader either and I make a kick ass commander," Meryn stuck her tongue out at him.

Magnus sighed. "Yes, dear."

A few minutes later the door opened and the ladies, followed by their relieved looking mates walked in. Vivi immediately went to Meryn and sat down on the sofa closest to her. "What do you need to know?"

"What exactly do the kids need?" Meryn asked.

Vivi blinked. "A cure?"

"No, like a medicine? What will make them better?"

"I'm trying to synthesize an antiviral that will mimic the antibodies found in someone who has been inoculated with the vaccine," Vivi explained.

"We're so close too," Ellie added.

Meryn frowned. "So, a person gets a vaccine and it fakes out the body into thinking it's sick then the body creates antibodies that fight off the fake sickness, right? Then when the real sickness comes along it doesn't affect them?"

Vivi nodded slowly. "Basically, yes."

Meryn pointed to Magnus. "Doesn't he have the antibodies? Can't you just use his blood?"

Vivi blinked up at Magnus. She then turned to look at Rheia and Ellie. "Could that work?"

Rheia and Ellie sat down next to Vivi on the couch. The three turned to face each other. Rheia nodded her head as she thought things through. "What about the transition markers?"

"They would have been neutralized by Serenity when she healed Magnus," Vivi answered.

"What about matching vampire bloodlines? We don't have time to use your stone," Ellie asked. All three turned to Meryn.

"You use your stone and another vampire's blood

to help prevent bonding and eliminate the need for an exact match, right?" Vivi nodded. Meryn continued. "And royal blood is usually intermingled with Noble blood, which is intermingled with citizen blood. Mr. Culpepper said that one of the reasons why it was such a big deal that the four royal houses were back is because nearly everyone in the city can trace their family back to those four houses." Gavriel, Magnus and Vivi nodded. "Well, Magnus has Gavriel's blood to give it a super boost." She eyed Vivi. "But your blood has all four houses since Gavriel and Caspian gave you some blood to heal your stomach. Wouldn't that make you like a universal donor for vampires and eliminate the need for an exact match?"

Vivi launched herself at Meryn wrapping her arms around the woman's neck. "I love you!" she peppered Meryn's face with kisses. "When this is over, come work for me!"

Aiden look dumbfounded. "Hold on, is she right?"

Vivi smiled and nodded. "There's no guarantee, but it's our best shot." She threw her head back and laughed. "DeLaFontaine thought he'd infect Magnus and get rid of him, but he effectively gave us the cure!"

"Wait! What about the children? Vampires are universal donors already for shifters, but what about bonding?" Ellie asked.

Magnus shook his head. "I do not care. I will watch over them all if I have to," he said emphatically.

"Vaccine, antibodies, old vampire blood but not from a vampire..." Meryn murmured looking up at the ceiling. Her head came down. "Colton! He's a wolf-shifter who received the vaccine, so he has the antibodies, but he also has Gavriel's blood running through him from when he got chomped on by the feral. So, he also has the boost of older vampire blood, but because he's a shifter you don't have to worry about bonding or the transition markers." She looked at Vivi. "He got Gavriel's blood about three months ago, do you think it would work?"

Vivi simply ran from the room. "Colton! Magnus! Hurry!" she screeched. Both men simply ran to catch up.

Adriel rose from his chair and walked over to stand in front of Meryn. Without saying a word, he practically bent in half bowing low to her. Grinning, Declan and Etain stepped up to bow to her on either side of Adriel.

Micah stood, leaned down and kissed her forehead gently. Silently he took a step back until he was beside Etain and he bowed low.

"Aiden they're doing that thing," Meryn said to her mate sounding upset.

"It's because you deserve it," Aiden said, his voice thick with emotion.

"Well tell them to stop. If they want to make me happy they can get me some meat kebobs or something," Meryn definitely sounded flustered.

As one, Micah straightened with his unit. Adriel knelt down on one knee in front of her. "Will you forgive me? I did not mean to discount the value of your input. My heart and mind were distracted by my concern for Micah. It is not an excuse, but I hope you understand."

Meryn just blinked. "So, am I getting meat

kebobs or not?"

Adriel chuckled and stood to ruffle her hair. She tried ducking from under his hand. "Cut it out!"

"I will fetch your meat kebobs whenever you like," he promised.

Meryn rubbed her swollen belly. "Maybe after some Magic Pudding."

"I will get some immediately," Sebastian said and disappeared from the room.

Ellie stood and helped Rheia up. "We're heading to the hospital. Knowing Vivi, she will take the injectors straight up there." Grant and Micah stepped next to the women. Micah looked back at Meryn. "If this works, I will owe you more than you know."

Meryn held up two fingers. "Two words. Meat. Kebobs."

"Absolutely," he said. "Anyone else coming?"

Kendrick and Anne stepped next to them. Kendrick met his eyes. "Us for sure. Anne can help with the children and I'll do everything I can to free Serenity of the spell."

Feeling impatient Micah turned toward the door. "Let's go."

It felt like centuries as they waited for Vivi to arrive with the different injectors, in all actuality, it was less than ten minutes. Micah stood next to his mate who was frozen in place in the center of the room, faintly glowing silver. Laelia and Radclyffe were on either side of the room helping the children. When they saw them enter, their hands dropped, and they rushed over to him.

"How can we get Serenity back?" Laelia asked.

"Meryn and the ladies think they have a workable cure. They'll be up here soon and the second the children are cured we'll be able to pull Serenity from the spell." He swallowed hard looking at his mate. Her skin had no color and a bright white streak of hair had appeared at her right temple. He reached out and touched it gently.

Fear gripped him as he turned to Kendrick. "She's out of time. There's hardly any magic left."

"Marjoram!" Vivi yelled, running into the hospital.

"We're here!" Marjoram met her in the middle of the room and divided up the injectors between herself, Rheia, Ellie and Anne. They ran to the little beds and started treating the children.

They had made it halfway down the row, when the first set of children began to have a reaction. Violent convulsions lifted their bodies off the bed and ripped them from their parents' hands as they tried to hold them down.

Suddenly the faint glow around Serenity disappeared and she fell forward into his arms. He knew before he lowered his head to her chest that her heart had stopped. "She's not breathing!"

Behind them the children continued to thrash, but his focus was on his mate. He would not allow her to go into the unknown alone. Heedless of the duties he was leaving behind he thrust his magic into her body, so he could follow her, where ever she was going.

"Micah! Pull your magic back! She'll take you with her," Kendrick yelled.

Micah tightened his arms around his mate and sighed happily. He could smell the sweetness of her skin, familiar and tantalizing. He threw open every channel of magic he had and was mildly surprised when earth magic responded. He had long ago given up on the ability. Without coaxing the green tendrils sunk deep into the floor. Through his magic he could feel it branching out, tiny roots fanning out over miles. Feeling sufficiently anchored he threw caution to the wind and rested his cheek against hers. Gods willing he'd see her again soon.

At first there was darkness, but in the distance, he could see a tiny figure. As he got closer he could see the outline of his mate.

"Serenity!" he called.

She turned looking confused. "Oh no! You head back this instant."

"No."

"No? What do you mean no? You have things to do Micah. You made a promise to Kendrick, you have to help our people."

"They'll be fine without me."

Tears appeared in her eyes. "Please my love. You'll forget about me soon enough. We only had a few days together. You have your kittens, and delicate flowers and dew drops to ease your pain. Please," she pleaded. "Go back."

He shook his head. "It is true, I have called hundreds of women kitten. Hundreds of dew drops and goddesses and delicate flowers. But I have only called one woman, my one and only, and that is you. An endearment that encompassed every hope, dream and desire I had for my mate. There is no me, without you. So, either we both go back, or we continue on to see what lies ahead."

"You stubborn goofball!" she whispered harshly.

"Your call, my one and only. Where do we go?"

"If Fate is willing to let me return, I want to go back. I want to experience every single moment she showed us. I want to carve them into my memory as they happen, and not have them slip away like a dream at dawn."

He took her hand. "It may hurt," he warned.

"Nothing worth having is easy. Besides, I can torture you later in repayment."

"I shudder in anticipation," he teased.

"Let's go."

He gripped her hand tightly and began following the now thick green rope securing him to the land of the living. Slowly they made their way toward the harsh white light.

Gasping he turned on to his side and began to choke. Next to him he heard a similar noise as someone else fought to breathe. Soft weeping came from all around them. He opened one eye to find that he was being held by the twins who had sweat dripping down their faces. He looked around for Serenity. Across from him, Kendrick sat on the floor with her cradled against his chest. Behind him Aiden, Colton and Gavriel lent him their strength. He let his head fall back to look behind Nigel and Neil. There his unit brothers supported the twin witches.

Now the thicker rope made sense. Kendrick, Nigel and Neil had used their earth magic to reinforce his anchor. They risked being pulled into the darkness to give him a chance to save his mate.

Kendrick glared at him breathing heavily. "If you ever try this again, I'll bury you before you stop breathing," he threatened.

Aiden bopped him on the back of the head. "He only did what any of us would do."

"Micah?" A weak voice called.

Micah pitched forward and started dragging himself along the floor toward his mate before Etain and Declan lifted him and carried him over to Serenity. They set him down and Kendrick gently lay her across his body.

He held her close as he leaned against Etain's legs for support. "Gods I love you so much."

She clutched at his shirt. "I am so mad at you right now. How dare you risk yourself," she said, her voice a mere whisper.

He tilted her head back and kissed her nose. "You promised to punish me later," he said.

"That's our Micah!" Declan exclaimed, plopping onto the floor visibly exhausted.

Serenity tried to look around but didn't have the strength. "The children?"

Ellie knelt down beside them, though her face was tear streaked her eyes were jubilant. "Meryn helped us figure out a cure. They're doing just fine." She looked over her shoulder where the children and their grateful parents looked on worriedly.

"How long?" Micah asked.

Kendrick tilted his head. "How long did it seem?"

Micah shook his head. "Minutes," he responded.

Adriel wiped his eyes. "You both were clinically dead for twenty-three minutes," he said in a shaking voice. "After Kendrick figured out what you were trying to do he called for the twins and they used their magic to help."

"They did help. If they hadn't, I think the thin string anchoring me would've snapped," he confessed.

"Of course, it would have snapped!" Kendrick growled. "Who uses an emerging power to anchor their soul to their body while they traipsed through the underworld!" he shouted.

Anne rubbed his shoulders. "There, there my love. They're back." Like their friends around them, her eyes were also bloodshot from crying and her cheeks were stained with tear tracks. "Don't you scare us like that again."

Micah knew he had just received his first order from his queen. He simply nodded before closing his eyes and resting his cheek on the top of Serenity's head.

"Okay people, let's get them both downstairs to the infirmary. That way you can visit whenever you want," Marjoram's practical voice rang out.

Micah fought to open his eyes. He saw Meryn standing behind her mate looking scared, nervous and pissed. She scrunched her nose up at him and sniffled. "You died."

"I was only mostly dead," he said and enjoyed watching her jaw drop. She covered her mouth as she chuckled. "I hate you right now."

"No, you don't."

"Come on," Etain said as he and Declan lifted him between them while Adriel carried Serenity.

Declan grunted. "How come we have to carry his heavy ass and you get to carry Serenity?"

Adriel looked at him flatly. "I outrank you," he said in a deadpan voice. "Now move out," he ordered.

"Tell Serenity not to freak out, but I'm going to rest my eyes for a bit," Micah told his friends.

"As long as you keep breathing I don't care what you do," Etain retorted.

"Put them here! I got the larger bed ready for them," he heard Broderick say.

He tried to give the man a thumbs up but was too tired. "Good looking out," he managed.

They gently placed him on the bed and set Serenity down next to him. He instinctively curled around her in a protective position. This time when darkness came he wasn't afraid.

Serenity stared at herself in the mirror. She braided the long white lock at her temple, a reminder of what she lived through. She flipped it back and forth. She still wasn't used to seeing it when she looked at herself.

She and Micah had technically died two days ago. When they woke up yesterday Vivi filled them in on everything they missed.

Meryn's idea worked. The shifters bounced back almost immediately but the vampires still slept. Vivi said that every time she took their blood, less of the virus appeared. She said it was only a matter of time before they woke.

Vivi also confessed to finishing her cure. Until they figured out who created the virus, they could use her synthesized antivirals to treat any future outbreaks. The best thing about her cure was that it required very little vampire blood and didn't have to be processed.

Vivi's voice was somber when she told her she finished it the night before. What she didn't have to say is that it would have been too late for her and the children.

"Serenity?" She heard Micah calling for her.

"Upstairs," she yelled back.

He appeared in the doorway holding a small cardboard box. "I got us something."

"What?" she asked.

He handed her the box. She looked up at him. "*Twister*?"

His eyes darkened. "One of my favorite memories from the night of our mating. Us laughing and playing naked *Twister*."

"Naked?" she asked feeling her body tighten in anticipation.

"Naked," he confirmed.

She pushed past him and ran to the large open space in their new master suite on Level One. It was still undecorated, but Micah wanted to stay close to his unit brothers. As she understood it, the other unit witches would be coming by next week to help them move everything down from the Unit Level.

She tore open the box and set the large mat on the floor. Micah set the dial to one side. Without saying a word, they each rushed to remove their clothing. Serenity knocked him over twice when he was trying to take off his pants. She was already laughing so hard she was having trouble breathing and they hadn't even started yet.

She stood naked in front of him playing with her breasts. "You going to go?"

Micah was staring at her hands. "Right." He shook his head and spun the dial. He looked down and placed his foot on a small blue circle.

Serenity deliberately bent over in front of him to spin for her turn. Behind her Micah whimpered. "Left foot, red." She chose the circle furthest from him.

"Hey!" he protested.

"Your turn."

Five moves later he somehow ended up behind her. When she got right hand, yellow she knew she was in trouble. Bending over slowly she placed her hand on the yellow circle.

She grazed up against him causing them both to groan. When last she looked his cock had been hard and leaking. She grit her teeth, determined not to be the one to give in.

"Y-y-your turn."

Using his magic, he spun the dial.

"No cheating!" she exclaimed.

"The rules state that I spin the dial, technically my magic is a part of me, so it's not cheating," he countered. His move had him bending over her to place his right hand next to her left.

All along her back his body pressed up against hers. She felt his hard length slide against her. She went to spin and gasped. She turned her head to glare up at him. "You've been using air magic to pick your moves!"

"I was wondering when you'd figure it out." He kissed the back of her neck. She felt his body shudder. "I almost lost you. You left me," he whispered.

She reached behind her and wrapped his arms around her body. "But you wouldn't let me go."

"I'll never let you go," he vowed.

She dropped to her knees then went to all fours. "Reclaim me Micah." When she looked back she saw his eyes had darkened. He stroked his cock from base to tip. "You belong to me," he said as he knelt behind her.

"Yours only. Forever."

She threw her head back in ecstasy as he plunged two fingers deep inside her. "Yes! Micah, please!" she begged.

He lined up the head of his cock and drove forward. There were no soft words or promises of tomorrow. It wasn't needed. She needed him in the most primal way imaginable. He wasn't making love to her, he was branding her. Claiming her as his own from the inside out.

She tilted her hips until he was hitting her g-spot with every thrust. She was so close, the sound of his flesh pounding against hers echoed all around them. She reached down and rubbed her fingers on either side of her clit. "Micah," she breathed.

"Mine!" he roared. She twisted her fingers and came harder than she ever had in her life. Her arms gave out, she would have pitched forward onto the floor, but he caught her and gently lowered her. He pulled from her body and slumped to the floor next to her.

"I love you Serenity."

"I know you do. No other woman has ever been loved the way you love me." She turned to face him and reached out her hand. Their fingers intertwined. She looked him in the eye. "I love you more than the promise of heaven."

His eyes filled. "Heaven still awaits us. But by the time we head there in truth, we will have accomplished all we set out to do in life. Our great-great-great-grandchildren will see us off and we'll go hand in hand. Together."

"Together," she repeated. "Forever."

"Forever."

CHAPTER THIRTEEN

MERYN SAT QUIETLY AT THE dining room table as conversations buzzed all around her. Everyone seemed to be talking at once. The children were virus free and the sleeping vampires were getting better by the hour. But something was off. Vivi checked in on Micah and Serenity and reported they were both awake and doing fine. Though it wasn't said out loud, everyone seemed to understand why they weren't at dinner. Meryn smirked, she'd be lucky to see those two before she left the city.

She leaned back in her chair as something continued to eat away at her. She just couldn't remember what it was or why it was important. Stupid baby brain.

"*Denka*, are you well?" Ryuu asked reaching for her wrist.

Around her the table quieted.

"Ryuu, is the child well?" Magnus asked.

Meryn stared at Rheia. What on earth had she said? Something about coming so far. Meryn gasped as she remembered why it bothered her.

They had come so far. Exactly down the path laid out for them, but by who?

"Meryn, baby?" Aiden took her other hand.

Meryn turned to Magnus. "You said I could have whatever I wanted, whenever, right?"

Magnus nodded. "You, more than anyone, deserves whatever your heart could desire."

"I want to speak with DeLaFontaine."

"No," Aiden said immediately.

She scowled up at him. "I didn't ask you."

She turned back to Magnus. "I wouldn't ask if it wasn't important."

Magnus gave her a soft smile. "I am beyond doubting you." He looked over to Adriel. "Secure him and bring him here. If she wants to meet with him, I want her surrounded by unit warriors at all times."

Adriel stood and motioned to Declan. "You are with me."

Declan grinned. "I knew you liked me best." Adriel was still ignoring him as they walked out.

Magnus stood. "Meryn if you would like to adjourn to the antechamber, I think you will be more comfortable there." He looked around. "And when he leaves we can return here without our dinner being spoiled by his presence."

"Dibs on the recliner," Meryn said standing.

Beth laughed. "I think it's pretty much yours now anyway."

Meryn let Aiden help her stand and escort her to the antechamber.

Quicker than she thought it would take, the door opened, and Adriel pulled DeLaFontaine into the room. When he saw Meryn, he snarled. "You!" he hissed. "Do not think I do not know that you were behind that humiliating spell."

Meryn frowned, then remembered the twin's diarrhea spell. She burst out laughing. "I actually had very little to do with that one, but thanks for reminding me. I needed a good laugh."

Adriel drove DeLaFontaine to his knees in the middle of the room facing Meryn. "He is all yours," he announced.

DeLaFontaine stared up at her. "What is this about?"

Meryn tilted her head. "I'm not sure yet. Something about you bothers me."

"He bothers all of us," Vivi muttered under her breath.

Meryn stared into DeLaFontaine's eyes. "Black, slick, oil," she said to herself.

She felt two hands come to rest on her back. She knew without turning it was Ryuu and Kendrick. "Keep going Meryn," Kendrick urged.

"I saw that black stuff again, with that Dubois douchebag, but not like him," she pointed to the man at her feet.

Meryn's gut instinct was proven correct when DeLaFontaine paled at her words. "Impossible," he whispered.

"You know what I think?" she asked him. "I think whoever is really in charge, the one who created this virus, I don't think they are kind enough to leave us an out. We did everything they thought we would do. We opened the city, we welcomed the refugees, we gathered blood, everything according to plan." Meryn raced after that one thought evading her. "Right up until I visited you. That's when I got those awful premonitions about Magnus. That was when we stopped doing what they wanted." She turned to Vivi. "What would've happened if I hadn't warned you about Magnus?"

Vivi frowned then swayed. Etain steadied her. "Magnus would have been strong enough, fast enough to either kill or incapacitate both Gavriel and Kendrick. Once wounded they would have been killed along with everyone in the room."

Meryn continued. "What would've happened if I hadn't stopped the third trial of older blood with the children and shifters on Level Six?"

Vivi covered her face with her hands unable to speak. Gavriel turned to Meryn. "The levels of testosterone in the blood from the transition markers would have reacted to whatever was in the virus to promote aggressive behavior. They would have gone feral. The adults would have hesitated to hurt them and they would have decimated everyone in the hospital." He stared down at DeLaFontaine. "Magnus would have started from the bottom and worked his way up and the children would have started from the top and worked their way down. Any victim who lost a mate would have also turned feral and the bloodbath would have grown at an exponential rate."

Meryn nodded. "That's what I thought." She stared at DeLaFontaine. "You're not smart enough to do all this. You're too self-centered. You would've wanted to preserve the city, so you could rule it, you wouldn't have created this." Her eyes narrowed. "Who is pulling your strings?"

DeLaFontaine's body slumped forward and his head hung down, his hair blocking his face. "Do you really want to know?" he asked sounding different.

"Yes," she replied.

"So be it," was the last thing she heard before light exploded behind her eyes.

"*Denka!*"

"Meryn!"

Shit, they are going to be so pissed at me.

Finally, she gave in to the pain.

When she opened her eyes, she looked round. She was standing in a bright white room. "Well fuck," she muttered.

A low masculine chuckle had her turning. "Holy shit!" she exclaimed. The man before her could not be real, he was simply too beautiful. If she weren't mated, she'd lust after this one.

"Thank you," he replied, in a deep voice. Silently he began to walk round her.

"Wait, can you read my mind?" she asked.

"In a way."

"Watch it, it can get a bit crazy in there," she warned.

He smiled and continued to circle her.

"I take it you're the head guy, the one in charge?"

"Something like that."

"Why are you doing all this?"

"Should you be asking so many questions? It cannot be good for your health," he warned.

"I've been asking questions my whole life buddy,

it's what I do."

"The witches warned me about you. You have no idea how long I have been looking for you."

"They warned *you* about *me*?" Around them a flash of blue light illuminated the frosted glass walls. She ignored it. "Why would you be looking for me?"

"I wonder how they kept you hidden?" he mused.

"Back to my other question. Why are you doing all this? Is it for the necklaces?"

"The necklaces are just a means to an end."

"What end?"

"Your world of course."

"Dude, seriously? You want to take over the world? Have you seen how fucked up it is lately? Trust me, it's a headache you don't want."

He stopped his circling to stand in front of her. "Imagine being locked away in a small, wooden box. There are no windows, no doors. It is dry, dusty, hot and confining. Would you not risk everything to feel a bit of fresh air on your face or taste sweet, cold, water?"

"I suppose," Meryn admitted.

"Even if it meant killing others?"

She shrugged. "Depends on whether or not they deserved it."

"You are not what I expected. Most humans would respond, 'I would never kill an innocent person,'."

"Most humans lie to themselves on a regular basis, I'm not that smart," Meryn said, wincing at another bright flash of blue light.

"You think more like a demon than a human,"

he complimented.

"Is that what you are?"

"Your Dark Prince will be able to tell you more," he answered. He eyed her closely. "You know. I was simply going to have you killed, but I may change my mind. You are amusing. I think we could have a lot of fun together."

"You know DeLaFontaine will be questioned by the council," she pointed out.

He gave a lazy shrug. "He has served his purpose."

"Whatever you're doing, if it hurts the people I care about. I will stop you."

"You can try, and I will enjoy watching you try." He smiled and held up a finger. "Wait for it."

Meryn shielded her eyes from another flash of light.

He laughed. "Your squire is losing his mind to get you back."

Now it was her turn to shrug. "I know."

He paused. "You knew that was your squire this entire time and you are ignoring him?"

"I told you. I ask questions, it's what I do."

He slowly approached her. She felt ice slide down her spine as his lips neared her ear. "And I kill people, it is what I do."

She turned so that their noses were nearly touching. "But you won't kill me." Of this she was sure.

He smiled and leaned back. "I may not have to."

"What do you mean?"

"Did I forget to mention? To speak to me, I had to stop your heart." His eyes were cold. "I did say that asking so many questions could affect your health."

Meryn's hand went to her belly. She raced to the glass and a door appeared traced in blue fire. She looked back. "This is your only warning. Don't piss me off."

He threw his head back roaring with laughter. When he looked back at her he smiled. "Ditto."

Meryn pushed on the glass until it gave way at the fiery seam. She tumbled forward into the blue light. She exhaled as warmth seeped into her body. She didn't realize how cold that room had been. In the distance she saw a hand reaching for her. She stretched as far as she could and let it pull her back.

"I have her!" Ryuu's familiar voice shouted.

"Dude, loud," she complained.

An ear shattering roar echoed around her. She opened her eyes and looked toward the sound. Adriel, Gavriel, Colton, Declan and Rex had a huge creature pinned to the floor. She smiled. "It's Fuzzy Aiden, come here boy," she said, holding out her hands.

The men toppled off the bear creature as it lurched forward to lay its head on her chest. "Aiden your freaking head is heavy, shift back or you'll squish our jellybean."

Slowly Aiden shrank back down, his clothes were tattered rags hanging off of him. Behind her Ryuu held her close to his body, refusing to let go.

She looked up. "You were the blue light."

His lips trembled, and his eyes were filled with

tears, but he did not let them fall. He simply nodded, unable to speak.

Aiden buried his face in her chest holding her belly protectively. "He killed you," he whispered in a guttural voice. When he turned to stare at DeLaFontaine's prone body his eyes were the solid black of his bear.

Meryn eyed DeLaFontaine and turned to Gavriel. "Take him back to the detention cells and seal it in a salt circle. Then come back up here for a family meeting."

Gavriel's eyes immediately flashed crimson. He hissed at DeLaFontaine before shaking his head. "It cannot be."

"You're the one who told me the stories, trust me, salt his ass then get back up here."

Gavriel moved quicker than she had even seen him move before. He had DeLaFontaine jerked up by his collar and out of the room in under two seconds.

Aiden snarled as his prey was taken from him. She kissed him on the lips. "I'm here and I'm not going anywhere I promise. I need you to pull your shit together for a bit. Later tonight you can examine every inch of me, but right now we have plans to make."

Aiden looked up at Ryuu. "She stays in your arms until I get back."

Ryuu nodded. "It shall be as you say." He tightened his arms around her.

Aiden stood on shaky legs and stumbled forward heading toward their bedroom. Colton and Adriel were at his side in seconds, propping him up on either side. "Come on Aiden, we will help," Adriel said, helping walk the drained commander to the bedroom to dress.

When she went to shift her weight Ryuu stilled her efforts. "Ryuu my back hurts. Can't you hold me in my recliner?"

"My apologies *denka*, I find that I am experiencing something very disturbing. It's a feeling I've never had before, and it is distracting me from my duties."

"Fear, Ryuu. What you are feeling is pure unadulterated fear," Kendrick said quietly from behind them.

Ryuu practically snarled. "I do not fear that creature!"

Kendrick placed a hand on the squire's back. "I never said you did." He looked down at Meryn. "I believe your fear stems from almost losing her."

"Oh, Ryuu," Meryn said softly. She reached up with both hands to cup his face. "I wasn't afraid you know. Because I knew you were there. You gave me the strength to face him." She wiggled until he let her get on her knees. Meryn didn't know if it was socially appropriate, but she always felt better when Aiden did it. Feeling unsure she leaned forward and kissed Ryuu on the forehead. "As long as we're together, everything will be okay," she promised.

Ryuu's mouth opened in pure shock. He looked back at Kendrick, as if unsure of his new emotions.

Kendrick laughed. "You cared for her, protected her, guided her. She is your charge, so you thought you could treat her like the others, but you were wrong. Unlike the others who only saw you as a tool to be used, she considers you family. She got past every barrier you ever created. What you are feeling is love, pure and simple. A love that goes past labels like squire and charge. She just stole a piece of your soul Ryuu," Kendrick clapped him on the back. "And it's about damn time."

Meryn dropped her hands and eyed Ryuu. "I love you, but do not want to have sex with you," she said plainly.

Her blunt, outrageous statement shook him from whatever stupor his emotions left him in. He took a deep breath. "And I love you too Meryn and do not wish to have sex with you either."

"You will still feed me, right?" she asked.

He gave her a flat look. "Of course I'll feed you. You'd probably try to sustain yourself on *Hot Pockets* again if I didn't."

Meryn exhaled in relief. "Thank god," she said then looked down at her wrist. "Hey! My tattoo changed! My dragon got wings!" She held up her wrist to Ryuu who was frowning. "That's not possible."

"He has wings!" she crowed getting to her feet. She held up her wrist hopping around.

"I thought I told you to keep her in your arms," Aiden growled as he walked back into the room. He scooped her up and nuzzled her neck. "Aiden! Look! My dragon has wings now!"

Aiden stared down at her wrist then over to Ryuu. "What did you do while I was getting dressed?"

"I kissed him on the forehead like you do to me all the time because it always makes me feel better. Then I told him I loved him, but I did stipulate I did not want to have sex with him," Meryn said rotating her wrist around checking out the new addition to her tattoo.

Declan nodded. "She was very clear about that part Aiden."

Ryuu gracefully rose to his feet. "*Denka* and I have moved to a deeper understanding of each other, which allowed us both to grow. I think the tattoo changing is a reflection of our new relationship." He straightened his vest and jacket before smoothing them to lay flat. He placed his hand over his heart and bowed. "*Denka*, if you would return to the dining table, I will continue to serve dinner."

Etain put his phone away. "Micah and Serenity are on the way. Normally I would let them rest, but I have a feeling they will need to hear what happened."

Meryn grabbed Aiden's hand and tried to pull him into the dining room. "Come on, I'm starving."

Magnus looked to the others. "Then by all means let us continue our dinner."

Micah gripped his mate's hand tightly as they hurried down the hallway on Level One toward the Rioux quarters.

"Did Etain say what was going on?" she asked.

"No, but he knew I wanted to spend more time reconnecting with you. It must be something important."

As they approached the entry door, they met up with Gavriel coming from the direction of the detention cells. His eyes blazed scarlet. He looked at them and simply nodded before opening the door for them to walk through.

When they walked into the dining room everyone was seated as they normally were, but the conversations around the table were subdued.

"I hid," Pip admitted quietly.

"I am glad you did Pip." Magnus said approvingly. "I did not want him anywhere near you."

Once they were seated Micah turned to Adriel. "So, what happened?"

Adriel simply drained his wine glass. Micah was about to ask Gavriel when he saw that he too was emptying his goblet.

Kendrick stared down into his wine, but wasn't drinking. That's how Micah knew it was bad. As a witch drinking impaired your abilities. If Kendrick wasn't drinking, he wanted to stay sharp in case he had to call on his magic.

Kendrick set his glass down. "Meryn confronted DeLaFontaine today and made certain truths clearer for the rest of us.

"The virus was designed so the only possible cure was older vampire blood."

Micah nodded. "We knew that."

Kendrick continued. "Meryn pointed out that, had we administered the third trial, bloodshed would have been inevitable as shifters and vampires alike lost control due to the aggression triggers built into the virus. I think we all realized the bullet we dodged, but only Meryn saw it for what it was. A calculated attempt to destroy the city."

"Father did not like that people were getting sick," Pip said quietly. "But the scary men said it was the only way father would get the city."

Meryn tapped on the table with her finger. "That's what I thought. He wanted to be the new prince, which meant he kinda needed people to kiss his ass. This virus would've wiped everyone out." Her eyes widened, and she looked over at Vivi. "I think because I stopped the trials, the city remained on lock down and they couldn't take advantage of the chaos to escape. So, your attack was simply a way to open the door for them to leave," she grimaced. "Sorry about that."

Vivi waved off her concern. "It wasn't your fault Meryn."

Aiden looked down at Pip. "Pip, why didn't you go to any of the unit warriors and tell them what was happening?"

Meryn glared at Aiden. "It's not his fault if he was scared of his dad."

Pip just blinked up at Aiden. "But the warriors knew."

Aiden looked over at Adriel who shook his head. Aiden turned back to Pip. "Why would you think that?"

Pip poked Aiden in the upper arm. "Because they had the same tattoos as unit warriors, except theirs were red."

Micah wasn't the only warrior to collapse back in their chair. Of course, Pip wouldn't know the difference.

Aiden had tears in his eyes as he continued to ask the questions no one wanted to hear the answers to. "Did they all have red tattoos?" Pip nodded. Aiden looked like he was going to be ill. "Is that why you tried to protect Meryn when we first met? You thought I was like them?" Pip nodded again. Aiden unbuttoned his sleeve and pushed it up to reveal his unit tattoo. "This is a unit warrior tattoo Pip. It shows what city, unit, and race we belong to. Mine is black because I am actively serving. When a warrior retires or goes inactive an outline appears around it." He swallowed hard. "When it turns red, that means the warrior has turned feral. Because warriors are trained for so many centuries it was decided that in the event a warrior loses his soul, the ink will turn red as a warning to others to stay away or call for help." He looked around the table. "There is nothing more dangerous than a unit warrior who has lost his soul."

Meryn covered her mouth with both hands. "The missing Vanguard."

Micah couldn't face the room. He buried his head in his arms on the table and tried to block out the truth. He felt his mate wrap an arm around him and hold him tight.

Finally, Meryn spoke, breaking the silence. "It explains the sophistication of this entire plan. The execution of it had military precision, not like the raging idiots we faced in Lycaonia."

Micah sat up and looked around at his fellow unit brothers. None of them wanted to contemplate taking down a single feral warrior much less two. From what Pip said the enemy seemed to have their own feral version of units.

Aiden had one hand over his eyes. "I need to call my father and tell him about the feral warriors. He will have to activate the Old Guard to help us deal with this." His hand dropped. "We will issue an edict making it mandatory for every unit warrior ever trained to check in and register for the app. It's the only way we can get a scope of how bad this really is."

"Why is this happening?" Ellie whispered, sounding completely hopeless. Grant scooted back and lifted her easily into his lap. She buried her face in his neck.

"The guy, who I think is a demon by the way, said that he was trying to get out of some kind of box," Meryn answered.

Ryuu looked down at her sourly. "You almost die and that is what you come back with?"

She glared at her squire. "This guy answered questions with questions, okay. I'm lucky I got that much out of him."

Gavriel looked to her. "Did he say anything else?"

Meryn looked up, recounting her experience. "I asked him if he was a demon and he said, 'The Dark Prince will be able to tell you more'. He said that the necklaces were a means to an end to get our world... Oh and witches warned him about me." She smiled. "Then he said he didn't think he was going to kill me because I was amusing, and we could have fun together." She frowned. "I think he likes me."

Hal appeared at Aiden's side and poured him a full goblet of amber liquid. With a shaking hand Aiden downed the whole thing and coughed once. He looked up at Hal. "Thank you."

Hal looked as spooked as the rest of them. "If anyone deserves a stiff drink it's you."

Kendrick held up a hand. "He mentioned

witches as in plural?"

Meryn nodded. "He said he wasn't able to find me because I was hidden or something."

Kendrick looked over to Gavriel. "By Fate?"

Gavriel shook his head. "At this point I feel like I do not know anything."

Kendrick turned back to Meryn. "How did you know to put a demon in a salt circle?"

Meryn brightened. "*Netflix*."

Kendrick's mouth dropped, and he turned to Anne. "Magic in your role-playing games, alchemy in anime and now demon hunting on *Netflix*? Why didn't I know about any of this?"

Anne's mouth twitched. "We can *Netflix* and chill later love." Meryn giggled, and Anne winked at her.

"How can you laugh?" Vivi asked. "How do we face tomorrow?"

Meryn tilted her head. "We face tomorrow because the alternative is to not face it, which means dying, and I for one, am not done doing all the things I want to do. Like, watching the newest season of *Doctor Who* or trying the new chipotle flavored *Cheetos*. I face tomorrow laughing, because if I let them steal my happiness, then they've already won, and fuck that, because I'm going to win."

Aiden sighed. "You could have said watch centuries worth of sunsets with my mate or tour the Amazon, but you went with *Cheetos* and *Netflix*?"

"Fuck the Amazon! Do you know how many bugs are in the Amazon? Like they don't even have an accurate count of the number of species there are, much less how many individual bugs. Did you know that one statistic says that in the Amazon, bugs outweigh all vertebrates four to one? Like imagine how many tiny bugs it would take to make up four of your huge ass. No way! Fuck that."

Aiden pouted. "I'm not that big Meryn and I don't have a huge ass."

Etain leaned in toward his mate and pointed across the table at the Unit Commander and his tiny mate. "That is how we face tomorrow. That is how we laugh. By finding joy in the moment." Etain's mouth twitched at Aiden's expression.

Serenity rested her head on Micah's shoulder. "We have thousands of moments to look forward to. We can't turn our back on all of them because we're scared of a few."

He turned to her and whispered. "I am especially interested in more naked *Twister* moments."

She blushed and kissed his temple. "You're on," she replied.

Kari sighed and picked up her iPad. "So, we have a possible virus creating demon leading an army of feral unit warriors, in addition to invisible reapers and mindless garden variety ferals?" She tapped a few times then looked up. Everyone was staring. "What? We might as well be organized about this."

Magnus was the first one to lose his composure. But his belly laughing seemed to trigger the entire room. They were facing impossible odds, but somehow being with family made it seem like everything would be okay.

Ellie sniffed. "What do we do now?"

Micah leaned forward to answer her. "Celebrate." He looked around the table and back to his mate. "Celebrate every moment."

Micah could see the unconditional love she

had for him in her eyes. "Because tomorrow isn't promised," she said smiling.

He raised her hand and kissed it. "But anything can happen, our future holds infinite possibilities and I intend to enjoy each one."

EPILOGUE

MERYN WATCHED THE CELEBRATION FROM her recliner in Magnus' antechamber. It was the day after their eventful dinner starring DeLaFontaine. Magnus went above and beyond hosting a huge party to celebrate the children getting well. Everyone was focusing on the good things, determined not to let the disturbing news weigh them down.

Micah and Serenity still had the recently mated glow about them, so the news of a possible demon must not be detrimental enough to burst their sex bubble. Meryn smiled. Who was she kidding? She'd been mated less than a year and she was still enjoying her 'honeymoon' phase with Aiden.

She eyed Micah's tee-shirt. Lifting her phone she took a picture and uploaded it to her *Pinterest* board so Dani could copy it later. The shirt simply read.

1692- Never again- Witches Lives Matter

She watched as Micah's mouth drop. "What do you mean it was Karen?" he asked.

Adriel held up his hands. "Do not shoot the

messenger. Dimitri told me to tell you that it was Karen and not to worry, he took care of it. He said after Karen found out Serenity helped to save those stricken by the virus she confessed to putting the snake in your laundry basket. Dimitri says she feels awful because her uncle was among those being treated at the hospital. He said she promised not to interfere with your mating again."

Serenity eyed her mate. "Who is Karen?"

Micah gulped. "Well, you could say she is past lover."

Serenity's eyes narrowed. "Your previous lover put a poisonous snake in your laundry to get back at me?"

Micah sighed. "The curse of being popular." He frowned. "I wonder why only Karen got upset?"

Serenity gave him an evil grin. "*Only* Karen? No *Twister* for you later."

His mouth dropped. "But Serenity..."

Meryn's attention was diverted from the Micah's pleading by the twins.

"Meryn!" Nigel called out, as he ran toward her, Neil, Pip and Avery right behind him. "We found some on Level Six!"

Meryn sat up straighter. "No way!"

Neil looked around the room before pulling out a small square object from under his shirt and placed it in her lap. The boys gathered round blocking her from view. Their heads all leaned down.

"What is it?" Pip asked.

Nigel watched Meryn intently as she unwrapped the brown paper to reveal a package of small cans. He looked at Pip. "Meryn was telling us about this drink. She said it was fruity like juice, carbonated like soda, but had all the wonderful effects of espresso." They all looked down at the magical liquid.

"This boys, is Sugar Free Red Bull. Normally I would rock the hell out of some sugar, but strangely enough the Sugar Free version tastes better than the regular one. It has more of a raspberry flavor." Meryn opened the package and handed each of them a small silver can. "You guys enjoy."

Neil frowned. "What about you?"

Meryn shook her head. "My little jellybean likes coffee, I don't want to tweak them out on Red Bull." She rubbed her belly.

Avery nodded. "That's probably a good idea." The four of them looked around and popped their cans. They took their first sips, looking surprised but pleased. It didn't take them long to finish their drinks.

"I don't feel anything." Nigel observed.

Meryn smiled. "Wait for it."

It hit Avery first. The small shifter began jogging in place. "This stuff is amazing, I feel like I can fly!"

Nigel and Neil stared. "Whoa," they said in unison.

"Fly? Really? Do you think it will help me?" Pip asked. "I mean it might help me. I should be able to fly, I am a vampire after all. I do not want to use this little stone forever." He looked at the twins. "Not that I do not think it is amazing. It really is. I just want to feel like I belong you know?"

"I think that stuff unlocked a new level in Pip's brain," Neil whispered.

Meryn laughed. "He isn't a video game."

Avery and Pip clasped hands and began swinging

each other around the antechamber.

"Pip, be careful you don't fling Avery across the room," Meryn warned.

"Okay," they both said together in a singsong voice.

Neil looked at Nigel. "Anything?"

Nigel shook his head. "Maybe it doesn't work on witches?" He sighed and Meryn heard a faint cracking sound.

"Nigel, I think it's working." Neil's eyes were locked on the stone under their feet.

The twins stared at the floor as flowered vines poured from the small crack.

"Wicked," they whispered in awe.

"Nigel! Neil! What in the gods' names have you done?" Kendrick bellowed.

"Weeeeeeeeee," Avery giggled, as Pip floated him up near the ceiling.

"Look Neil, Pip is flying! He's doing it!" Nigel pointed to Pip and Avery.

"Way to go Pip!" Neil yelled.

"Avery!" Warrick shouted. He stayed under his mate his arms out stretched in case he was dropped.

Meryn sat with her hands clasped in her lap watching as the boys had fun. Before meeting Aiden she never understood what 'family' meant. But she was slowly learning. Seeing the boys happy, made her happy.

Nigel and Neil ran from Kendrick and ducked behind Anne who laughed and shielded them from her mate.

"Kendrick, can you fix this?" Magnus asked, as the plants began to bloom.

Sebastian smiled. "I think it is a lovely addition."

Aiden walked over to Adriel. "Any word on how DeLaFontaine was killed?"

Adriel shook his head. "Marcus said he was asleep and didn't see anything. Leif and Travis swear no one entered the detention cells." He turned to Meryn. "Meryn do you think anything was captured by your cameras?"

Beside her Sebastian froze slightly as he serving up a large bowl of Magic Pudding. Meryn put on her most bored expression. "Nope, I checked the footage myself, didn't see a thing." She smiled at Adriel and Aiden who turned back to each other.

Adriel rubbed the back of his neck. "Maybe the demon killed him since he was not needed anymore," he suggested.

Aiden nodded. "I bet that is what happened."

"And just for Meryn an assortment of imported coffee infused chocolates," Sebastian said handing her the huge bowl of pudding. "If you give me just a moment I will get them for you." He leaned down and whispered. "Thank you."

She grinned up at him. "That was some of the sexiest shit I've seen in a while," she said laughing when he blushed. He straightened and turned to Ryuu. "She is simply adorable." He walked away whistling to get her chocolates.

Meryn wasn't lying. Watching Sebastian stroll into the detention cells past a dazed looking Leif and Travis had been amazing. Watching him use his power to force DeLaFontaine to snap his own neck had been mesmerizing, but the cold detached way Sebastian told DeLaFontaine he had sealed his fate when he went after his charge had given Meryn life goals.

Since DeLaFontaine had been scheduled to be executed Sebastian wasn't at risk of losing his soul. She happily munched on her pudding.

Ryuu nodded his approval. "He is a fine squire."

"Yup. Makes killer pudding too."

Meryn stretched her neck trying to see past Aiden when she heard a flurry of noise at the door. Sebastian hurried past her to welcome whoever had just arrived.

"Father?" Etain said incredulously. Meryn had to practically tip her head back to see all of the fae. He was huge!

The impossibly sized fae pulled Etain into a hug. "I had your brother, sister and mother stay in Eiré Danu. I was not sure how safe it would be after the portals opened."

Etain pulled Vivian forward. "Vivi, this is my father. Liander Aerlin. When he passed the role of head of household to me I became Vi'Aerlin, so his name reverted back to our core name," he explained. She nodded. He turned to his father. "Father, I have the honor to present my mate, Princess Vivian Vi'Aerlin. Even though she was born from two of the vampiric royal houses of DuCoeur and DuSang, she has chosen to take my name." He gently placed a hand over her abdomen. "She carries my child, a new fae life."

Liander's eyes widened. "A thousand blessings on you," he whispered. Then his face dropped and he turned to Etain. "Your mother and sister are going to kill me for making them stay behind." Etain simply laughed. Liander ignored him and placed a glowing hand on Etain's shoulder. "That should replace what you have lost."

Etain sighed. "Thank you, father. I feel much better."

Meryn's attention turned to Declan who looked scared of the man and woman in front of him.

"Mother? Father? What are you doing here?" Declan asked.

The smaller woman launched herself at Declan. "Where else would we be? Both of my sons were trapped in the city with a shifter virus spreading!"

"Father, I would like to present Kari Delaney." Rex pointed to her mid-section. "And that is baby Lionhart," he gushed.

The older version of Declan swept Kari into a huge hug. "Thank the gods you are well."

Meryn looked up at Ryuu. "I think the vampires woke up since the portals seem to be working."

"That is probably an accurate assumption *denka*," he replied.

The presence of family truly made the celebration complete. Sebastian, Pavil and Hal were truly in their element as they served and entertained so many guests.

"Here she is!" a male voice called.

Meryn looked up at Stefan. "Who are you talking to?"

Seconds later a slightly older version of Stefan stepped into view. His warm brown eyes smiled down at her. "So this is the female with the elusive scent?"

Meryn glared up at Stefan. "I do have a name you know."

"Meryn, I'd like you to meet my older brother Cristo Bolivar."

Cristo dropped down on one knee in front of

her so he wouldn't tower over her. He took her hand to shake it and frowned. He brought it up to his nose.

"He's doing the sniffing thing," she whispered to Ryuu.

Cristo's hand began to tremble under hers. She looked up at Ryuu. "I want Aiden," she said unsure of what was happening.

"I am here," Aiden said, taking her hand from Cristo's and stepping between them forcing Cristo to stand and step back.

"Cristo?" Stefan asked looking confused.

Cristo looked past Aiden. "Please," he begged. "Let me scent her just one more time. I have to be sure."

Aiden moved a fraction of an inch and Cristo popped around him. Though his hands trembled his eyes were filled with tears and wonder. "I don't wish to frighten you," he reached down for her.

Slowly she took his hand and he bent over to smell it again. When he straightened there was pure joy in his eyes.

"Yes! Yes! Gods! Yes!" He dropped her hand and began to dance around.

"Cristo, what in the hell?" Stefan demanded.

Cristo looked to Stefan. "Tell father he's in charge of the pack for a bit. If you want to find out why she smells familiar you have to come with me."

Stefan nodded. "Okay. Where are we going?"

Cristo ignored him and looked around the room. "Is Law Ashleigh here? I caught a faint whiff of his scent."

Law stepped out of the crowd that had formed around them. "I'm here you damn bloodhound.

What are you doing to Meryn?"

Cristo walked over and placed both hands on Law's shoulders. "Law Ashleigh I need you to invoke your emergency password and get Thane to Eiré Danu."

Law's eyes bugged out. "Look, I can't go into it, but we have a ton of stuff going on right now."

Cristo tightened his fingers. "Tell. Him. Drop everything and go to Eiré Danu." He stared into Law's eyes. "Trust me, he will want to be there."

Meryn held up her hands forming a 'T'. "Time-out! What in the hell is going on?"

Cristo knelt down in front of Meryn and took both her hands in his. "I want to tell you but I can't. I swore an oath that I would not speak of what I know outside the protection of Eiré Danu. Will you please come with me to the Land of Eternal Sun?"

Meryn searched his face. Like his father and brother he embodied a sense of truth and loyalty. She freed her empathy and what she saw convinced her.

"You're a shield for those behind you," she said.

He blinked back tears. "I try to be, sometimes I fail."

"After our party. Give me a few days to tie up some things here, then I will go to Eiré Danu." She shrugged. "The queen wants to meet me anyway."

Cristo stood. "Perfect! I'm going on ahead to get something out of storage. Gods! I hope I can find it." He kissed her forehead and grabbed Stefan by the arm. "Let's go find father and tell him he's Alpha again for a while."

"I didn't get any food!" Stefan complained as

they walked out the door.

Aiden stared down at Meryn. "What!"

She smiled up at him brightly. "Guess what baby? We're going to Eiré Danu!"

Thank you for reading!

I hoped you enjoyed MY ONE AND ONLY! For a full listing of all my books please check out my Official Website www.alaneaalder.com

I love to hear from readers so please feel free to follow me on Facebook , Twitter, Goodreads, AmazonCentral or Pinterest.

Hug me please!!

SEND ALANEA A
HUG!

LEAVE A REVIEW

If you liked this book please let others know. Most people will trust a friend's opinion more than any ad. Also make sure to leave a review. I love to read what y'all have to say and find out what your favorite parts were. I always read your reviews.

IMPORTANT!!

As you know Facebook strictly controls what shows up on your newsfeed. To ensure that you are receiving all my latest news and teasers you can to sign up for my newsletters so you will receive regular updates concerning release information, promotions, random giveaways and future Live events.

I typically send only 1–2 updates per month and won't flood your inbox, promise! ;)

OTHER BOOKS BY ALANEA ALDER

KINDRED OF ARKADIA SERIES

This series is about a shifter only town coming together as pack, pride, and sloth to defend the ones they love. Each book tells the story of a new couple or triad coming together and the hardships they face not only in their own Fated mating, but also in keeping their town safe against an unknown threat that looms just out of sight.

Book 1- Fate Knows Best
Book 2- Fated to Be Family
Book 3- Fated For Forever
Book 4- Fated Forgiveness
Book 5- Fated Healing
Book 6- Fated Surrender
Book 7- Gifts of Fate
Book 8- Fated Redemption

BEWITCHED AND BEWILDERED SERIES

She's been Bewitched and he's Bewildered…

When the topic of grandchildren comes up during a weekly sewing circle, the matriarchs of the founding families seek out the witch Elder to scry to see if their sons' have mates. They are shocked to discover that many of their sons' mates are out in the world and many are human!

Fearing that their future daughters–in–law will end up dead before being claimed and providing them with grandchildren to spoil, they convince their own mates that something must be done. After gathering all of the warriors together in a fake award ceremony, the witch Elder casts a spell to pull the warrior's mates to them, whether they want it or not.

Each book will revolve around a unit warrior member finding his destined mate, and the challenges and dangers they face in trying to uncover the reason why ferals are working together for the first time in their history to kill off members of the paranormal community.

THE VANGUARD
We Hold the Line.

Book 1- Inception

Made in the USA
Middletown, DE
10 July 2022